With Jake Maynard she no longer felt alone.

The realization slammed into Caro, fascinating and terrible. With him she felt different. More alive. Less alone.

It had to be because they had a common purpose, caring for Ariane. Except as the atmosphere stretched taut around them, she knew this wasn't about Ariane. It was about her as a woman and Jake as a man.

Did he feel this throb of awareness?

Caro couldn't afford to think so. Not with so much at stake. This masquerade. Ariane.

She couldn't risk her position here! She should run as far and fast as she could in the opposite direction.

But how could she leave when Jake looked at her that way? As if she were Venus herself, striking mortal men with yearning. A spark ignited deep inside that grew and grew as he ate her up with his eyes.

The old longing to be wanted rose again, her fatal weakness.

Growing up near the beach, **Annie West** spent lots of time observing tall, burnished lifeguards—early research! Now she spends her days fantasizing about gorgeous men and their love lives. Annie has been a reader all her life. She also loves travel, long walks, good company and great food. You can contact her at annie@annie-west.com or via PO Box 1041, Warners Bay, NSW 2282, Australia.

Books by Annie West

Harlequin Presents

Seducing His Enemy's Daughter
Inherited for the Royal Bed
Her Forgotten Lover's Heir
The Greek's Forbidden Innocent

One Night With Consequences

Contracted for the Petrakis Heir
A Vow to Secure His Legacy

Secret Heirs of Billionaires

The Desert King's Secret Heir

Passion in Paradise

Wedding Night Reunion in Greece

Royal Brides for Desert Brothers

Sheikh's Royal Baby Revelation
Demanding His Desert Queen

The Princess Seductions

His Majesty's Temporary Bride
The Greek's Forbidden Princess

Visit the Author Profile page
at Harlequin.com for more titles.

Annie West

———

REVELATIONS OF A
SECRET PRINCESS

HARLEQUIN
PRESENTS

HARLEQUIN®
PRESENTS®

Recycling programs
for this product may
not exist in your area.

ISBN-13: 978-1-335-14838-4

Revelations of a Secret Princess

Copyright © 2020 by Annie West

This edition published by arrangement with Harlequin Books S.A.

For questions and comments about the quality of this book,
please contact us at CustomerService@Harlequin.com.

Harlequin Enterprises ULC
22 Adelaide St. West, 40th Floor
Toronto, Ontario M5H 4E3, Canada
www.Harlequin.com

Printed in U.S.A.

REVELATIONS OF A
SECRET PRINCESS

This story is dedicated to Agnès Caubert,
Fabiola Chenet and all the other special women
who make up Les Romantiques.

Thank you for your friendship!

Thank you, too, for your work in hosting the
wonderful Festival du Roman Féminin and
for always making this visiting Australian feel
welcome.

CHAPTER ONE

CARO EMERGED FROM the café, huddling into her coat as the wind swirled around her ankles and bit her face. Funny that her skin could feel numb with cold while inside she was all churning heat. Nothing could extinguish that fire inside.

Except the possibility she might fail.

She faltered to a stop, grasping a lamp post with one gloved hand, fighting nausea.

Her head told her success was unlikely.

Her heart urged her on. Not with logic, but with desperate hope.

She'd never been courageous or adventurous. From infancy she'd been trained to do as she was told, never make waves or put herself forward. Her one attempt to break free and make her own decisions had been disastrous.

But that was years ago. She'd changed, reinventing herself in the aftermath of tragedy and pain. Caro might not be naturally intrepid but she was determined. She breathed deep, swallowing sharp, sustaining Alpine air. She'd do whatever it took now to succeed.

Caro looked up the street of the famous Swiss ski resort, ultra-exclusive with its astronomically high prices.

Tourists gaped at the elegant shop windows, but they'd be gone by evening, driven away by the chic resort's unaffordability.

Up a nearby valley was one of the world's most iconic mountains. In the other direction lay her destination. Setting her jaw, she crunched over a dusting of late snow and got into her small rental car.

Twenty minutes later Caro nosed the car around a bend and emerged in a cleared space that hung partway up a mountain. The view was spectacular but she barely noticed.

She'd assumed she was driving to a ski lodge or an architect-designed home positioned for a multimillion-dollar vista. Instead she looked up at a wall of pale stone, a fairy-tale profusion of towers with steep, angular roofs. There was even a portcullis, raised to reveal a cobbled courtyard.

Caro stared at the centuries-old castle. This was no romantic ruin. It looked solid and meticulously maintained.

She'd known Jake Maynard was rich but he must have money to burn to live here. Her research told her he hadn't inherited it. His permanent home was in Australia.

She set her jaw. Caro had seen behind the scenes of the rich and famous and knew human frailties lurked there as they did everywhere. Wealth and overt luxury didn't awe her.

That was the one tiny advantage she had. Caro clung to it, feeling the nervous lurch of her stomach, tasting desperation on her tongue. Slowly she drove under the portcullis with its security camera, feeling each bump of the old cobblestones. Then she parked in the corner of the courtyard, next to a sleek, black vehicle.

It was only when she switched off the ignition and heard the silence thicken around her that she realised her hands shook.

Firming her lips, she reached for her purse, flicked a look in the mirror and pushed the door open.

She could do this.

She *would* do it.

Two lives depended on it.

'Ms Rivage is here.'

At the sound of his secretary's voice, Jake reluctantly looked up from behind his desk. Neil stood in the doorway, his expression bland.

Logic had urged Jake to excise this woman from the shortlist. She didn't have the experience of the front-running applicants. Yet one small detail in her application had caught Neil's eye, and Jake's. Small but vitally important. He raked a hand through his hair and told himself he'd give her fifteen minutes.

Neil stood aside and she walked in.

Jake felt his eyebrows channel down in a frown, his senses humming like the rigging on a yacht when a sudden wind rose. The nape of his neck prickled and his nostrils flared as if sensing...something.

She looked like a nanny straight from central casting. Yet at the same time not. He surveyed her plain skirt suit, scraped-back hair and apparent lack of make-up.

What was it about her that didn't fit? He'd learned to rely on his instincts and right now they sensed... something.

He got to his feet and walked around the desk, hand outstretched.

'Ms Rivage.'

His hand engulfed slim, soft fingers, yet her grip was firm as she returned his gesture. Most of the other applicants had non-existent handshakes. Either they'd simpered up at him, or were content to let him take the lead. This one looked him square in the eye.

But only for a moment. Then her brown gaze slewed from his and he knew she stifled anxiety.

Of course she's anxious. She's applying for a job. She must know her qualifications aren't impressive.

Yet his sixth sense tickled, telling him this was more than interview nerves.

'Please, Ms Rivage, take a seat.'

She nodded. 'Thank you, Mr Maynard.'

Her voice was deeper than he'd expected, with a husky resonance that teased an altogether earthier part of his consciousness. Perhaps it was the hint of an accent colouring her perfect English. But Jake had never been swayed by a sexy accent. Not unless it was accompanied by an equally sexy body.

Caro Rivage's body was hard to define behind the boxy jacket and skirt. She was tall in those heels, just half a head shorter than he, and her long legs were slender. She subsided into the chair with a grace that seemed at odds with the sombre suit. Brown clothes, brown eyes, dark, dull brown hair. She should look forgettable yet Jake found it hard to drag his gaze away.

Maybe it was the neat way she angled her ankles beneath her, accentuating an innate femininity that plain suit belied. Or the creamy skin that contrasted so startlingly with the dark suit.

Not completely pale. His gaze traversed her small, lush mouth and high cheekbones, both tinted the palest pink. Not, he'd swear, from make-up. This looked like the genuine article, a peaches and cream complexion, unblemished by the years of sun exposure he was used to seeing in his fellow Australians.

She shifted, her eyes lifting almost to his, then away, making Jake aware he was staring. The knowledge disturbed him. He wasn't interested in Ms Rivage's skin. Even if it looked as soft as a petal.

He pulled out his chair and sank into it, sprawling comfortably. Again that swift almost-stare from his guest before she looked down and smoothed her skirt.

Was she afraid of men?

But then she lifted her chin and their gazes collided. He felt the impact as a wave of heat.

Jake stared back, intrigued. What was this sensation? Attraction? Surely not for such a sparrow, even if she did have nice legs and an intriguing face. Suspicion?

Something about her made him cautious.

'Tell me about yourself, Ms Rivage.' He leaned back, elbows on the chair arms, and steepled his fingers under his chin.

Jake Maynard's voice was a delicious rumble that she felt like a burr of pleasure in her veins. Caro blinked, ordering herself not to be fanciful. She was immune to male charm—once bitten, twice shy. Yet even as the thought surfaced, she knew this man wasn't trying to charm. Despite the gesture of welcome and the barest hint of a welcoming smile, she sensed an intensity of purpose that made her pulse quicken.

Or maybe it was the laser-sharp keenness of his grey eyes beneath coal-black eyebrows. It made his eyes seem diamond bright and knowing, as if he saw beyond her carefully constructed appearance to those secrets she hoarded close.

It took everything she had not to shift in her seat or betray any other sign of weakness. Or break away from that glittering stare.

She drew a deep breath, conscious of the unfamiliar new suit, the pantyhose and heeled shoes that felt so different from the comfortable jeans, skirts and flat shoes she'd worn for the past few years.

The very act of putting on these clothes made her simultaneously grateful for the camouflage and unsettled by the reminder of her other life.

One black eyebrow climbed his broad forehead towards thick, ebony hair, reminding her he was waiting. With that hard but handsome face, powerful physique and enormous fortune Jake Maynard probably wasn't used to women making him wait.

The thought dampened the worst of Caro's nerves, helping her focus. She'd been distracted by the aura of strength emanating from him, courtesy of broad shoulders. By even features and that slash of a dimple in one cheek when he offered his half-smile. By his air of strength and dependability.

As if any man could be relied on!

She folded her hands and began. 'My application speaks for itself. I love working with children and I'm very good at it. As you'll see from my references.'

Her chin lifted as if anticipating an argument. Even now her father's habit of squashing her self-confidence had its effect. She expected Jake Maynard to disagree with her claim, though it was true.

For too long those cool eyes held hers, then his gaze fell to the papers before him. Caro's breath rushed out in relief. She'd have to do better than this if she were to convince him and win the job.

The possibility of being rejected was unthinkable. She bit her lip as he looked up, brows contracting as he read her features.

'You don't have formal qualifications.'

'A degree in early childhood education?' She shook her head. 'My experience is all hands on. But you'll see I've done a number of short courses on specific early learning issues.'

He didn't bother to check her application again, letting it fall to the desk. Caro's heart plunged with it. Surely that wasn't it? He wouldn't write her off so easily, not when he'd decided to interview her!

'I have to tell you the other short-listed applicants have both practical experience, years of it, plus excellent formal qualifications.'

There it was, the brush-off she'd feared. Nausea churned at the idea of being given her marching orders.

'Have you read my references? I believe you'll find them persuasive.'

He sat back further in his chair, as if getting comfortable while he watched her squirm. He didn't bother glancing at her application.

Maybe the contrast between his bronzed skin and the dark jacket he wore teased her imagination, or perhaps it was his almost insulting air of indolence, but for a second Caro fancied something demonic in the knowing slant of those dark brows. Something fierce

and compelling and totally at odds with this comfortable room full of old, leather-bound books.

'I'm supposed to be awed because one of your ref-
erees is a countess?' Had he memorised her application? Caro was surprised he recalled that level of detail.
'Unfortunately for you, Ms Rivage, I'm not swayed by
an aristocratic title.'

His sneer rankled. Stephanie was a dear friend as
well as a client. She'd given her reference in good faith.
Caro sat taller, fixing her slouching interviewer with
a stare.

'The key part of the reference is the description of
my work, Mr Maynard, not my employer's title.'

Those straight eyebrows rose as if he was surprised
at her response. Did he expect her to sit silently while
he picked her application and her friends apart?

'Her son faced a range of difficulties when I began
working with him. Together we made considerable
progress.'

'You claim all his improvement was because of
you?'

'No. It was a team effort that included some spe-
cialised programmes. But I was there with him every
day, a major part of that.'

That might not sound as good as *I did it all myself,*
but it was the truth.

No sign of approval on those stark features. Maybe
that was how Jake Maynard looked while processing
information—gaze sharp, brow frowning and mouth
pursed. The expression emphasised the heavy planes
of his jaw and the slant of his high cheekbones. He reminded Caro of a picture that had fascinated her as a
child, of a medieval knight frowning in concentration

as he pinioned a flailing dragon the size of small Shetland pony with his lance.

Her sympathies had always been with the little dragon.

'You think four or five years working as a nanny and preschool assistant make you the best person to look after my niece?'

She'd been wrong. The steely glint in his eyes was more condescending than the medieval knight who hung in a dark corner of the upstairs corridor. It reminded her of her father's chilly stare. The one that through her childhood had reduced her to apologetic silence.

That, as much as her desperation, stiffened Caro's spine.

Slowly she shifted position, sitting back in her seat and lifting one leg, crossing it over her other knee, feeling the slide of silky pantyhose. A flicker in that grey-eyed stare told her Jake Maynard noted the movement.

For some reason her chest constricted, as if the air turned thick and hard to breathe. She refused to let it show, instead adopting what she hoped was a relaxed pose.

'I can't speak about the other applicants, but if I'm given the opportunity I'll devote myself to your niece totally. You won't have any complaints.'

'That's a big claim.'

'But true. I know my capabilities, and my dedication.' In that at least she was absolutely the best person for the job.

Her stomach plunged. He didn't look impressed. Why should he? No doubt he had hordes of ultra-qualified specialists at his beck and call. The very real possibility of being ejected without a chance to prove herself seemed more likely by the moment. Then where would she be? What other opportunity would she have?

Caro re-crossed her legs. 'Clearly you were interested enough in my application to interview me.'

Her pulse thundered in her ears as she stifled fear at the prospect of failing. She'd known her chances were slim yet she'd obstinately clung to hope. This was her one opportunity to make things right. If Jake Maynard had any inkling of why she was really here she'd be out of the door before her feet touched the ground.

The thought flushed heat through her, eddying deep inside and burning her cheeks. Was his niece somewhere close even now?

'Perhaps I was interested in meeting a woman so confident despite her lack of solid credentials.'

Caro stiffened. His tone hadn't changed, hadn't even sharpened, but his words were like harpoons piercing soft flesh.

Fortunately it took more than words or dismissive stares to discomfit her these days.

'I'm sure, Mr Maynard, you wouldn't drag applicants out into the wilds of the Alps on a mere whim.'

At least she hoped so. Surely this interview meant she had a chance?

'Wilds?' He shook his head. 'You object to the location? The advertisement made it clear this is a live-in position.'

If he was looking for an excuse to reject her it wouldn't be that.

'No, I'm quite content to live in the country. In fact it's what I'm used to.'

Silvery eyes bored into hers and Caro looked back

calmly. Her heart might be hammering an out-of-kilter tempo and her palms might be damp with nerves, but she wouldn't show it. Better to take the initiative.

'I understand your niece is from St Ancilla—'

'Who told you that?' He leaned forward abruptly, hands planted on the desk, as if ready to vault across the polished wood. Now she registered what his chilly expression had concealed. Protectiveness.

Maybe it was the innate caution of a wealthy, good-looking bachelor, a target for the paparazzi. Yet Caro sensed his protectiveness was for his niece. Caro warmed to him a little. She was glad the little girl had someone to stand up for her and keep her safe.

Out of nowhere emotion swept in, blindsiding Caro. It rose, a choking ball of heat in her throat, making her swallow convulsively. It roiled in her belly and prickled the backs of her eyes. If only she'd been stronger—

'Are you going to answer me?'

Caro blinked and met that searing stare, hating that moment of weakness. 'I did my research before applying for the position.'

For the first time since she'd walked into this room, Jake Maynard didn't look completely in control, despite his perfectly tailored clothes, his big desk and air of authority. 'That's not common knowledge.'

Fear rippled through her. Had she slipped up already? Her mind raced, thinking through what she'd said.

'It may not be common knowledge here, but in St Ancilla it's no secret.' She paused. 'The accident that killed her parents was reported by the local press.' When still he didn't say anything Caro continued. 'I'm very sorry for your loss. It must be a difficult time for you and your niece.'

Caro's heart squeezed. If her information was right, and she knew it was, little Ariane had been orphaned twice. Once as a newborn and then again a month ago when her adoptive parents died in a severe storm. The poor mite had had a rough start to life.

Caro was determined that the child's future would be brighter. In so many ways.

'And you somehow linked that small news item to my advertisement? I don't recall the St Ancillan press mentioning me.'

He sounded sceptical and she couldn't blame him. In fact he sounded downright suspicious.

That was the last thing Caro needed.

Jake Maynard was a self-made multibillionaire. You didn't become a world-class financier without being clever and insightful, or by taking people at face value. Why had she ever thought this might be straightforward?

The answer was simple. Because she needed it to be.

She smoothed her hands over her skirt, buying time to conquer her emotions.

'A friend lives in that part of St Ancilla and happened to mention that you were now Ariane's guardian.' Caro paused, hearing the slight wobble in her voice as she said the little girl's name. Stupid to let emotion affect her now. She couldn't afford any sign of weakness. This man would pounce on it mercilessly. She looked straight at Jake Maynard and spread her hands in an open gesture. 'Later, when I saw your advertisement I put two and two together.'

'I see.' He leaned back again and she tried not to

let her gaze drift to those imposing shoulders or that strong jaw. 'You do get around, don't you? First in St Ancilla, now in Switzerland.'

Why couldn't Jake Maynard be easy-going and friendly? Eager to employ a nanny from Ariane's island homeland in the Mediterranean?

Caro met his gaze with the polite smile she'd perfected as a child. The one her father had approved when she needed to look happy for the press.

She had no intention of admitting she only knew of Jake Maynard's search for a nanny because she'd been seeking a chance to meet Ariane. Let him think she was in Switzerland for some other reason.

'Fortunately both air travel and the Internet are available to many of us now, Mr Maynard.'

A hint of a smile turned up the corner of his mouth and for a second Caro saw a glimmer of appreciation in that hard gaze, making it look almost warm. The effect was startling.

She sucked in a slow breath, to her consternation feeling her bra scratch flesh that suddenly felt over-sensitive. Deep inside flared a kernel of heat that had nothing to do with nerves. It felt like feminine awareness.

Caro told herself she was imagining things. She was immune to men.

'You think I should give you the job because you come from the same country as my niece?'

She brushed her sleeve, giving herself a moment's respite from that searching gaze.

'I think it's useful that I speak the language and understand the culture. Such things are comforting, especially at a time of loss.' She paused. 'Even if she's not going to live there, there's a strong argument for her keeping her native language.'

Slowly he inclined his head, as if reluctant to agree. 'Frankly that's the only reason you're here, Ms Rivage. Because Ariane needs someone who can speak Ancillan as well as English. She's lost her parents but I don't want her to lose her heritage too.'

His voice hit a gravel note and something shifted inside her. For the first time since Caro entered this imposing library she felt real sympathy for the man before her. His expression hadn't altered yet that tiny crack in his voice hinted at deep-buried grief.

He might remind her of a sexy fallen angel with that blatantly raw masculinity and a simmering impatience that bordered on arrogance, but he'd recently lost his sister and brother-in-law. Plus inherited responsibility for his niece.

He probably wasn't at his best.

'I have some experience of dealing with loss, Mr Maynard. If you give me the chance I'll do everything I can to support your niece and help her thrive.'

His eyes held hers and for the first time she sensed he wasn't quite so negative. Was it wishful thinking?

She didn't have a chance to find out for there was a tap on the door and it swung open.

'Sorry to interrupt, Jake, Ms Rivage.' It was the secretary, Neil Tompkins, who'd escorted her upstairs. 'There's a call I really think you need to take. The Geneva consortium.'

Jake Maynard pushed his chair back. 'My apologies, Ms Rivage. This is bad timing but it's crucial I take this.'

Even so, Caro gave him credit, he didn't simply march out, but waited for her response.

'Of course, Mr Maynard.'

'I won't keep you long.' Then the pair disappeared, the studded oak door closing behind them.

Caro shot to her feet as if from a catapult. Sitting under that icy scrutiny had taken its toll. Leaving her bag beside her chair, she paced the room, drawn to the incredible vista of snowy mountains, so different from her Mediterranean home.

Her mind raced through what he'd said and how she'd responded. What she could have said better. What she could say to sway him on his return.

If the other applicants were so much more experienced it was unlikely he'd entrust his precious niece to her. On the other hand, Ancillan wasn't a common language. Its origins were ancient, with roots in classical Greek and even, the linguists thought, Phoenician, but influenced over the centuries by trade and conquest so it had traces of Italian, Arabic and even Viking borrowings. If she was the only applicant who could speak it she had a chance.

The door banged open and Caro swung around. But it wasn't Jake Maynard who entered, nor was it the door to his secretary's office that stood open. It was a door on the other side of the room.

In front of it, poised as if in mid-flight, was a small, dishevelled figure. Her frilly dress was rumpled and her plaits were half undone so her head was surrounded by a bright bronze nimbus of curls.

Caro's heart stopped.

She breathed. She must have, for she didn't black out. But she couldn't move.

Memory swamped her as the little girl turned a tear-stained face and drowned violet eyes met hers.

Caro felt a trembling begin in the soles of her feet and work its way up her legs to her hands and belly. She swallowed then swallowed again, unable to moisten her suddenly arid mouth.

She'd struggled, hoped and prayed for this moment. But nothing had prepared her for the raw shock of reality.

Those eyes. That hair.

She was thrown back in time to her own childhood. To the only person in the world who'd ever loved her. To gentle hands, tender words and a thick mass of curls of the same distinctive burnished bronze.

'Where's Uncle Jake?'

The little girl's words dragged Caro back to the present. She tried to smile but her mouth trembled too much. Her knees gave way and she sank onto the padded window seat, her hand pressed to her middle as if to still the tumult inside.

'He'll be back in a minute.' Her voice was barely audible, rough with emotion.

The girl's eyes widened. 'You speak like me!'

Caro hadn't realised she'd spoken Ancillan.

Then the girl she'd come all this way to find, the girl she hadn't known about till a few weeks ago, slowly crossed the room towards her.

Caro went hot then cold as relief, disbelief and wonder hit. She was torn between the urge to grin and the need to sob.

Or to gather Ariane close and never let her go.

CHAPTER TWO

OBLIVIOUS TO HER distress, Ariane stopped before her and held up a teddy bear that looked worn and well loved.

'Maxim's arm came off.' Her bottom lip trembled as she held up the separated limb. 'Can you fix him?'

It took Caro a moment to follow her words. She was so busy taking in the heart-shaped face, wide eyes and smattering of tiny freckles across that little nose.

Despite all the evidence Caro had told herself it was possible there'd been a mistake. Things like this—long-lost relatives and scandalous secrets—didn't happen in the real world.

But face to face with Ariane, doubt disintegrated. Those eyes, that hair, even the shy, questioning tilt of the head, were unmistakeable. Was it possible for a child to inherit a gesture, a way of holding themselves, if they'd never spent time with their birth family?

The impossible was real. Real and here before her.

Searing emotion smacked Caro in the chest. She gulped a noisy breath, unable to fill straining lungs. Her eyes filled—her first tears in years.

Instantly the little girl backed away.

That was possibly the only thing that could have helped Caro get a grip, the sight of Ariane retreating.

From somewhere Caro conjured a wobbly smile.

'I'm sorry. I didn't mean to scare you.' She lifted a hand to her eye, blinking back the unshed tears. 'I think I had something in my eye. Now, tell me about your bear. He's called Maxim?'

Ariane nodded but kept her distance.

'That's a fine name.' Caro resisted the urge to move closer. She'd already upset the poor kid with her tears. It would do no good to rush this, though instinct urged her to wrap her arms around the child and hold her tight. 'Did you know there was once a king called Maxim? He was very brave. He fought off the pirates who tried to invade St Ancilla.'

Ariane took a step nearer. 'That's where I come from.' She tilted her head. 'Are you from there too?'

'I am.' Caro let her smile widen. She'd never allowed herself to imagine having this conversation, as if it might tempt fate into obliterating all her hopes.

This was a bittersweet moment. Sweet because after all the grief and years of emptiness, Caro had found the girl she hadn't known about. Bitter because of those wasted years.

But there was no time for dwelling on past wrongs. Suddenly Caro had never felt more alive, more brimming with excitement.

'What happened to Maxim? Was he in a battle with pirates too?'

Ariane smiled and Caro felt it like a dart of sunshine piercing her heart. 'No, silly. There aren't really pirates.'

'Aren't there?' Caro stared at the bright face with the dimpling cheeks and felt her insides melt.

Ariane shook her head. 'No. Uncle Jake said so.'

'Ah, I see.'

'So don't be scared if you dream about them. They're not real.'

'That's good to know. Thank you.'

Did that mean Ariane often had nightmares? Again Caro resisted the impulse to gather her close.

Ariane tilted her head, clearly curious. 'Who are you? You look…' her forehead scrunched in concentration '…like someone I know.'

Caro's heart thudded high in her throat. 'Do I? Who do I look like?'

She shook her head. 'I don't know.'

Caro drew in a slow breath, reminding herself Ariane was a little girl. She imagined Caro was familiar, possibly because they were from the same place. Maybe speaking Ancillan made her seem familiar. There was no more to it. Anything else was impossible, even if Caro felt the connection between them as a tangible bond.

'What happened to Maxim if he wasn't fighting pirates?'

Ariane pouted. 'I don't know. I woke up and he was like this.'

Caro eyed the bear, with its fur rubbed off on one side where he'd clearly been cuddled a lot. She'd guess Ariane usually held him by that arm and the stitching had given way after much use.

'That's easily fixed.'

'It is?'

'Of course. All we need is a needle and thread to sew him back together.'

Ariane stepped closer and held out the brown bear and his separated arm. 'Can you fix him now? Please?'

Those huge eyes in that grave little face would make any heart melt. As for Caro, it took everything she had to keep things light.

'I don't have any thread with me but we can patch him up till we get some.'

'Patch him?'

'Yes. If you get my bag from near the desk I'll see what I can do.' Because even now her knees felt too wobbly to take her weight.

She watched the girl dart across the room. Obviously Maxim was a much-loved bear. Who'd given it to her? Her parents? Her Uncle Jake?

Caro thought of the self-contained man who'd interrogated her across the desk and tried to imagine him with this precious little girl. She couldn't conjure the image, but that didn't mean he didn't care. He was protective of Ariane.

'Here.' She held out Caro's capacious bag.

'Thank you.' Caro barely stopped herself calling the child by her name. 'My name is Caro. Can you say that?'

'Caro. That's easy.'

'And what's your name?'

'Ariane.'

'What a pretty name.'

'My daddy said he and Mummy picked it because I was so pretty.' Those big eyes filled with tears and Ariane's chin wobbled.

Caro's excitement shattered, her insides curdling. Ariane had lost her parents. She was grieving.

'I can see that,' Caro said slowly as she reached for her bag and began to rummage in it. 'I know some girls in St Ancilla who are called Ariane. They're named for a famous lady. She was very pretty, but more importantly she was kind and brave too.'

'She was?' Ariane blinked up at her, diverted.

'Oh, yes. She lived a long time ago before there were good hospitals and medicines. When all the people were very sick from a bad illness the lords and ladies shut themselves away because they were afraid they would get sick too. But Ariane came out of her castle and visited the poor people. She made sure they had food and clean water and helped them get better.'

'I want to be like her. I want to help.'

'Well,' Caro said slowly, withdrawing a scarf from her bag, 'you can get some practice now, helping Maxim. Here. Can you hold his arm like this?'

Ariane nodded and stood by Caro's knee, head bent as she concentrated on holding the bear and his arm in just the right way. Caro felt the brush of her soft little hand. A flutter of sensation rippled up Caro's arm, arrowing to her heart. She tugged in a tremulous breath and focused on fashioning the scarf into a sling.

There'd be time for emotion later, when she was alone. She couldn't give in to it now. That would be self-indulgent, besides scaring a child who knew her only as a stranger.

But as Caro knotted the scarf, her attention wasn't on the bear but on Ariane, whose world had been ripped apart. Who needed stability, kindness and above all love.

Caro vowed that, whatever it took, she would be the one to provide that.

* * *

Jake stood in the doorway, watching the pair with their heads bent over the teddy bear.

There was nothing especially arresting about the sight. Yet there was something about the woman and the girl together that hit him like a fist to the ribs.

Because it should have been his sister Connie here with Ariane?

Jake released a slow breath from searing lungs.

That went without saying. He'd give everything he had to see Connie here, alive and well. But this skitter of preternatural awareness didn't spring from loss. Or not loss alone.

What was it about this pair that stopped him in his tracks?

They spoke Ancillan so he didn't understand their conversation. Yet he'd understood Ariane's sadness and the way Caro Rivage had directed the conversation, allaying the tears he'd seen brim in his niece's eyes.

His confidence in this woman as a potential nanny soared. Anyone who could make Ariane smile these days was good in his book. He liked Ms Rivage's sensitivity, the deft way she'd handled what looked like a fraught moment.

Not that he was ready to give her the job. Her qualifications were laughably light compared with some of the experts who'd worked in the field for decades.

Jake frowned, watching her wind something around the teddy's arm, murmuring to Ariane.

There was something there he couldn't put his finger on. Some...similarity between them. His nape prickled as instinct stirred.

It wasn't their colouring. Ariane's was vibrant

whereas Caro Rivage had dull brown hair and dark brown eyes. Ariane's face was heart-shaped and Caro Rivage's was oval. Yet the slanting set of their eyes looked similar and maybe something around the shape of the nose.

He shook his head as his brain cleared. There *was* no link. It was merely the way they worked together, both intent, both speaking Ancillan. He imagined things.

For some reason his sixth sense had worked over-time ever since Caro Rivage arrived. So much that after the phone call he'd checked her application again at Neil's desk, looking for anomalies. But there was nothing that didn't fit. The references and qualifications of all the shortlisted applicants, including Ms Rivage, had already been checked.

His first assessment had been right. She was ordi-nary, not outstanding.

Jake always chose outstanding. He didn't have time for ordinary. That was how he'd built his busi-ness and his personal fortune, through excellence. Yet he couldn't stifle the idea that perhaps it wasn't out-standing Ariane needed but someone ordinary. Some-one to help her grope her way back to normalcy after her trauma.

He frowned. That was crazy. He wanted the best for Ariane.

Jake ploughed his fingers through his hair. Maybe he was oversensitive when it came to choosing Ariane's nanny. This wasn't like his usual decisions. Then there was nothing at risk but money, albeit lots of it.

Where his niece was concerned, Jake refused to take risks. She'd been through enough. He thought of his sister and brother-in-law's car, crushed almost to nothing by a massive tree brought down in a storm. It was a miracle Ariane had survived when her parents died.

He owed it to her and Connie to keep her safe.

He stepped into the room. Instantly the woman in brown jerked her head up, those impenetrable eyes locking on his.

What was it about her that made his hackles rise?

Clearly, despite her apparent absorption in the child, she was attuned to his presence. Jake didn't know whether that was good or suspicious.

Or maybe, the idea surfaced again as their eyes held and his chest expanded on a deep breath, it wasn't suspicion tugging at him. Could it be attraction?

Jake dismissed the idea. Caro Rivage might have fine features and a certain understated elegance, and poise...definitely poise. But Jake preferred more in his women. Eye-catching beauty and scintillating personalities for starters. Jake didn't date dull sparrows.

Nor did he mix work and pleasure. No dating the staff.

He stopped before them, jaw firming. She wasn't staff. Not yet. Probably never.

'What happened to Maxim? Is he okay?'

Ariane looked up and he caught a fleeting smile. His niece was pleased to see him, even if not pleased enough to hug him. He stifled a pang of regret.

He couldn't blame her. He was still almost a stranger. His trips to St Ancilla hadn't been frequent and though he'd stayed with Connie and her family, he'd usually worked during the day when Ariane was awake.

'His arm came off. But Caro can fix him. We need...' She turned to the woman.

'Thread. Wool to sew his arm on.'

Ariane nodded. 'Wool. Do you have wool, Uncle Jake? Please? Then we can make him better.' Pleading eyes turned to him and Jake felt that familiar stab of discomfort.

It was crazy that he should be responsible for this needy child. What she required was someone who knew how to care for her. Someone who could fill the gaps he, with his lack of experience, couldn't.

'I'm sure we can rustle some up.' He hunkered near his niece, enjoying the way she smiled back, clearly delighted with his news.

What he hadn't counted on was discovering the surprisingly rich scent of the woman holding Ariane's teddy bear. Jake's nostrils flared as a hint of her warm, spicy fragrance reached him. It was the perfume of a sensual woman, not heavy but far more intriguing than the predictable floral scent he'd have expected of a prim sparrow. He inhaled deeply then wished he hadn't as his sense receptors shuddered into awareness.

Jake shot a look at her under lowered brows but she avoided his gaze.

Because she felt that jag of awareness too?

Grimly he yanked his brain back to order. There *was* no awareness.

'I'll call Lotte and we'll see if she has any wool, shall we?' The ever-efficient housekeeper would have some, or be able to acquire it.

'And a needle please, preferably a large one.'

Up close Caro Rivage's husky voice sounded surprisingly sensual. Was she trying to entice him into giving her the job? She was in for a rude awakening if she thought he'd be swayed by a sexy voice.

Yet once more when he looked she was all but ignoring him. Instead she smiled at Ariane as she put the teddy into the little girl's arms.

Jake stared, amazed at how that smile turned this passably pleasant-looking woman into someone almost...stunning. The joy in her expression could be bottled and sold as a tonic.

As if sensing his stare, she darted a glance at him then away, fussing over the sling she'd arranged.

'Please, Uncle Jake. Can you ask now?'

'Of course.' He got up and called Lotte on the house phone. The interview had been derailed by Ariane and her damaged bear. But perhaps that was a good thing. Despite requiring the best qualified person, he also had to find someone caring. Someone Ariane could relate to.

As he watched the two females together it seemed as if he'd found just that. Or, he amended, someone who could put on a good initial show but who might not have the depth of experience Ariane needed. The thought loosened the ribbon of tension tightening around his gut.

He didn't *want* to give Caro Rivage the job.

Yet there was no denying Ariane liked her. He owed it to his niece to give the woman a chance, despite his doubts. Without a solid reason to reject her she deserved that much.

Ariane spoke again.

'Can you speak English, Ariane?' that throaty voice asked. 'I don't think your uncle understands Ancillan and it's not nice to exclude him.'

Spoken like a true governess. As if he cared. He

was just glad to hear Ariane sound so animated after weeks of being withdrawn and teary.

'Exclude?'

'It means to shut someone out so they feel all alone. It's not a friendly thing to do. You don't want to hurt your uncle's feelings, do you?'

Ariane shook her head yet she looked unhappy. 'But I like talking with you. It's like being home, talking with my...' Her mouth clamped shut and her little chin wobbled and Jake wanted to tell her he didn't give a damn what language she spoke. He hated it when she withdrew into that grief-stricken bubble where he had trouble reaching her.

He opened his mouth but Caro Rivage spoke first. 'Of course you want to speak Ancillan. I'm sure you'll soon be able to do that a lot.'

'With you?'

Jake's heart cramped as he looked into that woe-begone little face.

'We'll have to see, won't we?' Full marks to Ms Rivage for not playing on Ariane's desperation to make promises she couldn't keep. She turned to the opening door. 'Now, is this Lotte?'

Jake crossed his arms and leaned against the desk to watch proceedings. As expected, Lotte had wool in several colours, plus needles and scissors. The housekeeper reached for Maxim, offering to sew him better, but she was forestalled by Ariane, who insisted Caro do it.

He saw the women's gazes meet, assessing and something more. Caro asked permission to use Lotte's supplies, then sought a second opinion on the choice of colour and needle size. By the time the two had discussed possible stitches and the need to reinforce Maxim's other arm, the women were firm allies.

Silently Jake applauded Caro Rivage. She knew she trod on the housekeeper's territory and had adroitly co-opted her as an ally rather than a rival. Lotte fretted over Ariane like a broody hen with a single chick yet now she smiled and nodded, praising the newcomer's stitching and telling Ariane that Maxim would be as good as new.

Caro Rivage was a smooth operator, able to read people's sensitivities.

Was that what she tried to do with him? Were those downcast eyes a ploy to make her seem the ideal nanny?

But she'd met his gaze steadily when she had to. He sensed she really was nervous, despite her show of calm. Clearly she wanted this job badly.

Was she broke? Her clothes looked new if unremarkable. Maybe she wanted the kudos of working for him. A stint in his employ would open any door to her.

The idea eased his tension. Why shouldn't she want the job? This vague sense of something askew dissipated. The woman checked out. She had no criminal record and her references were good.

'Maxim looks as good as new,' he murmured when she cut the thread and handed the bear to a grinning Ariane.

'Thank you, Caro!'

Jake thought Ariane might even hug the newcomer, but instead she cuddled the toy while Lotte looked on, beaming from ear to ear.

Jake cleared his throat. 'Perhaps, Lotte, you could take Ariane for a snack while Ms Rivage and I conclude our business?'

It took some doing as Ariane didn't want to leave but finally they were alone. He watched Caro get to her feet. Her hands twisted together before she seemed to collect herself and let them fall to her sides. Her eyes met his and once more he felt the curious blankness of that dark-eyed stare. It struck him that when she was in control of herself she gave little away.

Jake was torn between annoyance and admiration.

'Shall I sit by the desk again?' She gestured to where she'd faced him across the expanse of glossy wood.

'No, Ms Rivage.' That deep voice rippled across her skin. 'The interview is over.'

Just like that dismay slammed into her. Her belly knotted with nausea. Caro flexed her fingers then linked them behind her back rather than press them to her roiling abdomen.

He couldn't dismiss her so quickly! They'd barely begun to talk when they'd been interrupted.

'I believe you should reconsider, Mr Maynard.' There. Her voice was even, though a little hoarse. Amazing what desperation could do.

'Reconsider? You haven't heard what I have in mind.'

Amusement sparked in his cool, grey eyes as if delighting in her discomfort.

Outrage filled her. She'd been the butt of her family's amusement so often as a child that it grated. Because she was shy. Because she looked different. Because she didn't fit with the rest of them.

Okay, it was mainly her stepmother rather than her half-brothers who'd made her feel an outsider, but the wounds carved deep. Especially as her father had merely raised his eyebrows and told her not to be sensitive.

Caro planted her feet more firmly and met Jake Maynard's sparkling gaze with one of her own. 'Perhaps you'd like to inform me what you *do* have in mind?'

Her tone would have done her father proud. Cool, composed and superior. She saw Jake Maynard's eyes widen then narrow suspiciously but she refused to back down. This was too important. This meant everything.

'I had in mind to invite you to stay overnight. To give you a trial period with my niece.'

Caro felt the air whoosh from her lungs, leaving her gasping for breath. Only years of training at projecting the right image kept her on her feet, for her knees trembled like leaves in a gale. Her heart jammed up in her throat and there was a roaring in her ears, blocking out the rest of his words. She saw him speak, tried to focus and heard something about this not being a promise of employment.

'Well, Ms Rivage? You haven't said anything. Does that mean you're not prepared to stay?'

Caro shook her head, buying time while she found her voice. 'No, Mr Maynard, it doesn't mean that at all. I'll happily stay tonight and get to know Ariane.'

'Good.' He nodded but didn't smile. In fact he didn't look happy at all, though he was getting his own way.

Perhaps he was so used to everyone jumping to do his bidding he didn't consider how inconvenient it might be for a job applicant to make an unscheduled overnight stay. Fortunately Caro had the suitcase she'd brought to Switzerland in the car downstairs.

'Very well. I'll have my secretary draw up a simple

agreement to cover us both in the event of any accident or liability during your stay.'

He really was a businessman through and through. Caro wouldn't have thought of that. But then she was in such a whirl she was barely capable of digesting what he'd said.

She watched him walk out of the door, heard the murmur of male voices in the outer room and reached out a hand to anchor herself. Her fingers clutched fabric and she blinked. She was grabbing the thick curtain as if it were all that kept her upright.

Caro sank onto the window seat, reeling. She felt hot and cold, anxious yet ecstatic.

She had a chance.

A chance to be with Ariane.

Her long-lost daughter.

CHAPTER THREE

'No, NO, EVERYTHING'S under control, Mr Maynard. The young lady is excellent with her. It's good to see your niece smiling.' Jake heard the relief in Lotte's voice over the house phone.

Because, with a temporary nanny here, she had time to get on with her own work uninterrupted? No, that wasn't fair. Lotte had a soft spot for Ariane. He knew she was pleased to see the little girl happy.

As he was. Even if he wished Ariane responded as enthusiastically to him as she did to this stranger she'd only known a few hours.

Catching his thoughts, Jake scowled. He wasn't jealous. The idea was preposterous. He thanked Lotte and hung up.

'Dramas?' Neil looked up from his laptop.

'Apparently not.'

His secretary nodded. 'I thought so. I had a hunch about her—'

'So you said. But you'll forgive me if I refuse to rely on hunches where Ariane's concerned.'

Jake wanted solid evidence that the woman would be good for his niece. A couple of hours keeping her content wasn't enough to tip the scales in her favour. Not against the other applicants.

'You don't like her?'

Put that bluntly, Jake felt almost ashamed to realise he *wanted* Caro Rivage to fail. Because of some inexplicable hunch of his own.

He shook his head. He trusted his instinct. It had saved his life in his long-ago army days. Listening to it had proved invaluable since moving into finance too, where sometimes the truth behind a too attractive investment could have sunk him if he hadn't raised questions.

'I'm reserving judgement.'

He told himself it was true. He summed up people quickly, not having time to waste. But with this woman he found himself still guessing. Perhaps his inability to read her made him suspicious?

Usually women were easily read. They liked his money, his power, his body, or perhaps all three.

Jake's mouth twisted. How had he ever thought Fiona, his last lover, different? Because she'd lasted longer? It wasn't much of a recommendation. He didn't miss her and felt a judder of distaste when he thought of her. Her attitude to Ariane had sealed her fate. Now she was back in England with her privileged friends or perhaps cruising the Riviera, searching for his replacement.

Amazing that he'd considered even for a second being with her long term. Her double-barrelled surname and cut-glass accent, her knack of knowing anyone who was anyone at society events, should have pressed every hot button. He despised trust fund hangers on, expecting life to give them what they wanted.

But she'd seemed so natural, down to earth and appealing. He'd been blinded by her quick mind, sense of humour and great sex.

Maybe his sister had been right and he'd begun to hanker after more than casual affairs. Fiona had been on the same page with that. She'd had the nerve to talk about Ariane being an unnecessary encumbrance when he, they, started a family.

The Honourable Fiona Petrie-Mathieson was a snob. Instead of helping when he found himself responsible for a grieving child, his lover had focused on the fact Ariane was adopted. She'd called her an anonymous baby, saying she could have been anyone's. The Honourable Fiona didn't want to pollute herself with ties to a child who didn't come from class or money. She'd suggested Ariane would be better with others of *her sort*, at an orphanage school Fiona *happened* to hear about.

As if Ariane weren't his sister's child and his only living family.

'No need to look so fierce, boss.' Neil raised his hands in mock surrender.

'Have I been giving you a tough time?' Jake leaned back and raised one eyebrow.

His secretary grinned. 'On a scale of ten? Let me think…'

Jake grunted out a laugh. They'd worked together for years. Neil could take anything he dished out and was no pushover. He also had a quick, analytical brain.

'Do *you* like her?'

'I told you she'd be good for the job.'

'Not what I asked. Do you *like* her? Trust her?'

Neil's amusement faded. 'You really *are* concerned!'

He paused. 'I've barely spoken to her. She seemed…
nice. Trying not to show she was nervous while she
waited for the interview. But I felt she was genuine, not
ignoring me because I'm a lackey nor buttering me up
for information about you. And she has a sweet smile.'

Jake shook his head. 'A sweet smile? Good thing
I'm hiring the nanny, not you.'

Neil shrugged. 'You asked. I like her better than the
one with two Masters Degrees. That one might know
the theories of child development but I'm not sure she'd
cope with a carsick kid.'

Jake thought of that eye-opening car trip through
the Alps when he discovered Ariane didn't travel well.

'You have a point.' He shoved his chair back. 'I'll
leave you to finish up. I'm going to check on this
would-be nanny.'

Jake was at the door when Neil spoke. 'There was
one other thing I noticed about Ms Rivage.' He turned
and caught the gleam in his secretary's eyes. 'She has
spectacular legs.'

Those legs were on display when Jake reached Ariane's
playroom. Rugs lined the floor and padded window
seats held bright cushions and dolls. But it wasn't Ariane or her room that snared his attention. It was Caro
Rivage standing on a small stool, arms raised above
her head as she reached for something on a high shelf.

Neil was right. She had spectacular legs. Fabulous
legs.

She'd taken off her shoes and stood on tiptoe, the
stance accentuating the fine curve of her calf. She'd
removed her jacket. Jake saw it draped over the back

of a nearby chair. Her white blouse strained over her breasts.

Something dug into his belly, grabbing tight. His nostrils flared on a quick inhale. His gaze tracked down to her toes and up over the loosely fitted skirt to a lithe torso revealed by that taut blouse. Then up the long, feminine arch of her tilted neck to her bundled-up hair.

Jake's breath expelled in a rush that left him almost light-headed.

Stripped of her conservative shoes and unflattering jacket, Caro Rivage was slim, svelte, feminine and intriguing. A different sort of intriguing from the way he'd viewed her earlier.

Except Jake knew that was a lie. Despite her prim pose and drab clothes, he'd been aware from the first of this woman's magnetism. It was a sly thing. Not overt like Fiona's blonde beauty and overtly sexy curves.

Even as he'd catalogued and dismissed Caro Rivage's expertise, at another level, that of primitive male, he'd been aware of the attractive woman behind the pursed lips and downcast eyes.

Heat drilled down from his temples to his gut, boring straight to his groin.

Did this explain his resistance? Was it why he didn't want to employ her? Because he responded to her as a man to a woman, not a boss to a governess?

He sucked air into tight lungs. Business and pleasure didn't mix. He had no intention of beginning anything personal with a staff member.

After Fiona he'd found it easy to avoid the charms of the opposite sex. Except, to his horrified fascination, he realised sex was the operative word here.

Caro Rivage bit her lip, shifted her hips in a way that shouldn't be in the least provocative yet turned up his inner thermostat from hot to scorching. The tug of desire dragging at his groin told its own story. It wasn't one he wanted to hear.

But Jake prided himself on facing facts.

She wasn't gorgeous like the women he dated. She wasn't his type. He hadn't decided if he could trust her, yet he was attracted.

Urgently attracted.

Worse, he felt compelled to give her a chance despite his better judgement because his niece showed every sign of bonding with her. That rankled. Jake made a point of being the one to dictate terms. He didn't take kindly to being forced into decisions. But little Ariane had held herself aloof from everyone except her teddy since the accident that killed her parents. Seeing her shy excitement with Caro Rivage was a profound relief. It was the first time she'd smiled properly in a month.

What option did he have but to give this nanny a chance?

She expelled an exasperated breath that puffed up the strands of brown hair drifting free of her brutally neat bun. She looked ruffled and pink-cheeked and Jake knew a growing curiosity to see her flushed and rumpled for other reasons.

'Can I help with that, Ms Rivage?' His voice hit a resonant baritone note that betrayed the trend of his thoughts. He could only hope she wasn't as adept at reading men as she was little kids.

His deep voice came out of nowhere, lassoing her around the middle and drawing her off balance. Caro

teetered on her toes, arms windmilling, then warmth
enveloped her. Hard warmth that wound around her
and held her steady.

She registered a broad palm and long fingers splayed
across her hip bone. A solid body, all heat against hers,
and near her breasts a head of tousled dark hair.

She hauled in a shocked breath and wished she
hadn't. This close she could smell Jake Maynard's skin,
warm and scented with bergamot and citrus. Her eyes
sneaked shut for a self-indulgent moment, enjoying
that fresh, masculine tang.

He was Ariane's uncle. A potential employer. An
obstacle to be overcome. She couldn't think of him as
a desirable man.

She hadn't considered any man in that way for years.
Not since she'd been blindsided by Mike's smiling at-
tentiveness, then gutted by his betrayal.

Reluctantly she looked down to Jake Maynard standing with his head a whisper away from her breasts.
Dark brows contracted over brilliant grey eyes that
no longer looked icy. Instead they reminded her of the
heat haze she'd seen rising over boiling geothermal
pools in Iceland. Heat drenched her skin and sank into
her bones.

Still she shivered.

'You can let go. I'm not going to fall.'

She wondered if he heard her, though his gaze was
anchored to her face.

'Even so. I'll get whatever you need. I'd rather you
didn't take a tumble.'

His voice was brisk, his movements quick as he
lifted her off the stool. Yet when he'd swung her to the
floor he took his time releasing her. Caro was inordi-

nately conscious of the weight and size of those hands. Of his tall frame, close enough to lean into. Of the tendril of beckoning male scent in her nostrils.

She stepped back smartly and he dropped his hold.

Belatedly she looked at Ariane, who'd turned back to the puzzle on the floor. Was it just Caro who felt the air thicken and clog when Jake Maynard was around? It must only have been seconds since he strode into the room yet it felt as if time had spun out far longer.

Panic whispered through her but she conquered it. She was stronger than this. No man would derail her plans.

'Thank you, Mr Maynard.' She pointed to the top shelf. 'There's a puzzle we wanted to try. If you could reach that one I'd be grateful.'

Of course he grabbed it easily, as she would have if he hadn't taken her by surprise.

'You like puzzles, Ariane?' Instead of handing it to Caro he crouched next to his niece. Caro registered the tautness in his folded frame as he waited for Ariane's response, and the ease of tension when she nodded and whispered that yes, she liked puzzles.

That was when Caro guessed some of his diamond-bright hardness might be down to something other than a demanding nature and a short temper.

Was he worried about Ariane? His movements as he settled himself beside the little girl were ostensibly easy, yet Caro saw how carefully he moved, as if not wanting to spook her. And though Ariane didn't move away, nor did she lean against his big frame. She didn't burrow close for reassurance as would be natural if she relished the comfort of a beloved uncle.

What was Jake Maynard's relationship with his niece?

As Caro put away the footstool and tidied a few toys, she observed them. Both were wary, treating each other with the politeness of strangers.

Caro huffed out a relieved breath. At least Ariane wasn't afraid of her uncle. If she had been... Well, she didn't know what she'd have done but she wouldn't have been able to watch without taking action.

The urge to declare herself and her relationship with Ariane was almost overwhelming.

Caro imagined announcing the truth, at which point little Ariane would fling herself into her waiting arms and it would be as if they'd never been apart.

Then what? Jake Maynard would simply relinquish his niece to her care?

She didn't even have to look at the obstinate angle of his jaw to know that wouldn't happen.

It was a nice fantasy but it would never be that easy. Announcing the truth would be complicated, especially since she had no intention of letting Ariane be taken from her again.

If she declared herself now she'd upset Ariane, who wouldn't understand why a strange woman claimed to be her mum. Plus she'd infuriate Jake Maynard who'd chuck her out of his castle before she could draw a second breath.

He'd think her mad.

Even if he didn't, if by some miracle she managed to convince him, he wouldn't let her stay. She'd seen his distrust and his protectiveness of his niece. If he had an inkling of the truth, she doubted she'd see Ariane again till they'd been through the mill of lawyers and courts. That could take years.

Caro pinched the bridge of her nose, tasting the rust tang of blood where she'd bitten her cheek.

She should have made a plan before coming here. A sensible plan with actions ready for every contingency. Instead, when she got this opportunity she'd sped here, needing to see Ariane.

Though it went against every instinct, Caro had to be patient. To wait, gain Ariane's trust and her uncle's. To work out how best to approach this.

Even if Jake Maynard didn't have a close relationship with Ariane, he cared for her. Caro guessed she was only here now because she and Ariane had connected. Not, she sternly told herself, because of their blood ties, but because they shared a common language.

It was ridiculous to think Ariane sensed their link though to Caro it was so blatant, so strong, she almost expected a fanfare and bright lights, as if a contestant on a TV show had won a fortune.

Abruptly the enormity of the situation hit her in slicing blows to her knees and stomach. She pressed her palm to her belly. There was a searing sensation inside, as if her baby had been ripped from her womb.

Caro's knees folded but she caught at a chair and collapsed on its cushioned seat. Ariane half lifted her head, looking for her, then, satisfied she was nearby, turned to Jake Maynard, pointing out something on the puzzle spread across the floor. Fortunately he was turned away from her. She hated to think of that intense scrutiny on her now.

Caro breathed through the pain, telling herself it wasn't real. There could be no physical pain now. It was well over four years since she'd gone through labour and an excruciatingly difficult childbirth.

But though her rampaging pulse slowed, the pain persisted.

It was the ache of loss, familiar because she'd endured it so long. Strange to feel it now when for the first time she had hope for the future.

She breathed deep, absorbing the fact that she'd found her daughter.

It was a miracle.

Caro had never let herself believe it possible. The idea that her baby was alive somewhere without her had been the fraught stuff of nightmares, taunting her till she awoke tearful and distressed, to the real world where such things couldn't happen.

Except it had.

Her jaw clenched and pain spiked from her grinding molars. She knew who was to blame.

Her hands curled into fists that trembled with the force of her emotion. Slowly, each joint aching with effort, she smoothed her hands on her thighs, feeling the bunch of stressed muscles beneath the fabric.

One day there'd be time to think of confronting the person responsible. Not today.

Her gaze slewed to the bright head bent over the puzzle and her heart lurched.

All that mattered was that she'd found her baby. That she was with her. She'd do whatever it took to stay at her side. And she wouldn't let anything, including Jake Maynard, stand in her way.

* * *

Jake forked his fingers through his hair, leaning back in his chair and rolling his shoulders. He'd had enough for tonight.

Trying to make progress with this new scheme was like wading through treacle in cement boots. He'd thought it easier to do business in Switzerland where he could access the principals in person, and he'd been right, to some extent.

He swivelled his chair, surveying the tapestries on the thick castle walls. His lips twisted. A medieval castle was a far cry from his usual surroundings.

The exclusive location meant he'd been able to entice some of the key players to this ultra-private retreat after the international summit in the next valley. That had provided impetus to his plans, but not as much as he'd like. There was a lot of work to do.

He wanted to stay in Europe to see how Ariane went. He'd thought of taking her back to St Ancilla for a visit. He was torn between thinking it could ease her pain and fearing it might send her back into the blank state of shock she'd been in at the hospital.

She needed time and he needed expert advice. Meanwhile, they'd stay here. This castle, rented from an acquaintance, was as good a place as any to keep Ariane from the media limelight. If any more intruding journalists turned up he'd simply drop the portcullis.

Jake turned and noticed a scrap of wool on the floor. It must have fallen when Ariane's bear was mended.

His thoughts zipped from his niece to the woman he'd invited to stay overnight.

He couldn't quite believe he'd done that when he

hadn't offered the better qualified applicants such a chance.

He got to his feet, shoving his hands into his pockets.

Caro Rivage had no criminal record and her references checked out. She was what she seemed, a woman who liked kids and had some experience with them. A woman well-regarded by her employers.

Yet something about Ms Rivage gave him pause. If only he could put his finger on it.

But how could he send her away after seeing Ariane's smile? The way she chattered with the woman, eager to be with her.

Jake stretched and looked at his watch. Almost midnight. He switched off the child monitor, knowing from the silence that Ariane was sound asleep. But he always checked on her before turning in.

Minutes later he reached Ariane's room. In the dim illumination from a nightlight he saw her curled up, thumb in mouth and her other hand hooked around her teddy. Jake's heart tugged.

She might not have been born Connie's daughter but Ariane was as much his niece as if his sister had carried her for nine months. Seeing the love in his sister's eyes for the tiny red-headed bundle, Jake had loved her from the first too.

He vowed he'd do better for her from now on. The first four and a half years of her life he'd been so focused on his projects that he hadn't spent enough time with his family, stopping by for quick visits and relying on long-distance calls to keep up to date.

Because he hadn't realised Connie would be ripped away.

That familiar pang filled Jake's chest as he thought

of his older sister, moving across the world to be with the man she loved. After her early years of struggle it had been a relief to see her settled with a nice bloke.

Jake turned, ready for his own bed, and his gaze caught a figure sitting in the corner. A figure he hadn't noticed because it was as still as the massive, carved wardrobe behind it.

The hairs at his nape sprang to attention. His scalp prickled and even the hairs on his arms lifted.

Caro Rivage could have been a statue. Her absolute stillness was uncanny. As was the way her gaze fixed so intently on Ariane.

It wasn't surprising to see a nanny in a child's room but surely not like this? Suspicion stirred.

'What are you doing here?'

She jumped, her hand flying to her chest as if to hold in her heart. Her face swung wide-eyed towards him.

Instantly his urgent protectiveness of Ariane faded.

He'd never seen someone look so vulnerable. Her dark eyes were…haunted. Her mouth gaped and her chest heaved as if she'd had the shock of her life.

This wasn't the expression of someone up to no good, but of someone utterly defenceless. Jake saw a terrible starkness in her face. Then her expression smoothed. She rose and crossed the room.

Did he imagine a pulsing charge of energy as she stopped before him? He frowned, thrown by the flight of fancy. Nevertheless, once more his senses stirred into overdrive in her presence. It was unlooked for and disturbing.

'I was checking Ariane.'

Jake darted a glance at his niece, still sleeping, then

jerked his head towards the door. When they were in the hall he scrutinised the woman before him. The light was better here but it was impossible to interpret her expression. She looked self-contained, as if presenting an unreadable front came naturally.

Again his sixth sense twitched a warning.

'A glance would have told you she was settled. You looked as if you'd been there for some time. Why?'

Something stirred, a fleeting expression, and Jake realised how pale she was, how tightly she held her mouth. His gaze lowered, past a fast-flickering pulse at her throat to the enveloping jacket and skirt. She hadn't even been to bed?

She swallowed and something jerked in his belly as he watched her slender throat work, feeling the tension vibrate off her in waves.

Now, instead of suspicion, Jake felt concern. He was familiar with pain and he recognised its shadow in this woman's unnaturally still features.

'What is it, Caro? What's wrong?'

'Nothing's wrong.' Her lips curved in an unconvincing smile. 'I wanted to check Ariane before I went to bed. She's going through a difficult time and something she said made me think she was prone to nightmares.' She spread her hands in a wide, helpless gesture that told him more about her state of mind than her face did. 'Truly, I just wanted to make sure she was safe.'

Her words rang convincingly and for once instinct told him it was true. She *was* here out of concern for Ariane.

True but not simple. That awful vulnerability he'd glimpsed in her momentarily unguarded face, that wealth of emotion had bordered on anguish. It couldn't be about Ariane, whom she'd only known a few hours. So it had to be about another child. A child she'd cared for and lost? Cot death? Illness? Accident? The possibilities were endless.

Pity rose, a rush of sympathy that made him want to comfort her. He moved closer then stopped himself.

'Get some sleep. My room's next to Ariane's so I'll hear if she wakes.' Maybe if he gave her this job she'd sleep near Ariane too, but he hadn't yet made that decision.

She nodded. 'Goodnight, Mr Maynard.'

'Goodnight, Ms Rivage.'

When she'd disappeared from view he exhaled slowly, thrown by what had happened. He'd wanted to haul Caro Rivage into his arms and hold her close. To ease the grim shadows that rode her.

His nostrils flared and he stepped back into Ariane's doorway, glancing at the curled-up child.

Tonight had revealed several things.

Caro Rivage was serious about caring for his niece.

She carried some distressingly heavy burden.

And he, with no real knowledge of the woman, without even wanting her here, had been on the verge of easing her pain with his arms around her and his lips on that inviting pink mouth. He wanted to hear her sigh with delight instead of anguish. He wanted her to smile at him with the warmth she bestowed on his niece. He wanted...

No. She was *not* his type. He wasn't interested.

Yet he'd stood mesmerised by the gentle sway of her hips till she disappeared from view.

He'd been right. Caro Rivage spelled trouble. Yet for Ariane's sake he wouldn't turn her away.

Ariane's sake?

With a snort of self-disgust Jake turned and stalked into his bedroom.

CHAPTER FOUR

'I'M SORRY I don't have better news, Caro, but this situation is a minefield.' Despite the early hour, Zoe's voice was crisp. No doubt, as one of the finest lawyers in St Ancilla, she was used to cutting to the heart of complex issues. 'This is likely to become a protracted court battle unless the two parties come to agreement.'

Her words fell like sharpened blades, slicing the sinews at Caro's knees. She grabbed the carved post of her four-poster bed, letting it take her sagging weight.

She'd been excited when she saw who the caller was, hoping Zoe had rung because she'd found a simple way through what promised to be a legal nightmare.

Her lips twisted. Since when had anything in her life gone as she'd hoped?

Wishing for something wouldn't make it happen. A happy family, a man who'd love her for herself, a future with her precious child—she'd dreamed of them all but not one had become real. No matter how hard she'd tried.

Caro set her jaw. This time it *would* be real. No matter what it took.

Beyond the window was a magical vista of soaring

mountains and sparkling, fresh snow. So clear and pristine. So different from the mess she found herself in.

'But surely the adoption wasn't legal? How could it have been when I didn't consent?'

She closed her eyes, her mind swimming with memories that had haunted her for years. The exhaustion, the blur of pain and fear, punctuated by moments of startling clarity when she realised something had gone badly wrong with the delivery. Her growing distress, and then…nothing, just blankness as the drugs took effect.

'That's something I'm trying to investigate. It's proving difficult.'

Caro dragged in a deep breath. She understood what Zoe wasn't saying. The impenetrable wall of denial and obfuscation that would meet her attempts to discover more.

Caro's father had pulled strings to arrange the adoption. He was a man adept at getting his way and as far as she knew no one had ever had the wealth, the will or the power to hold him to account.

Till now. In this he'd gone too far.

Sometimes, in her more desperate moments, she considered confronting him and calling him to account. Except she knew it would be like a gnat biting a bull. He'd swat her aside and immediately turn all his considerable power to making the problem go away. Then she'd be up against two powerful men, not one. Better to bide her time, for now.

'Difficult or not, there must be a way forward.' She bit her lip. 'I want to avoid a long court battle, for Ariane's sake especially.'

'It appears both sides can argue a legitimate claim to the child.'

She's not 'the child'. She's my daughter!

Caro clenched her teeth against the instinctive protest. Zoe was only doing her job, telling her the legal reality.

'My advice is to talk to her guardian. Negotiate. See if you can find common ground.'

Negotiate with Jake Maynard? The man was a world-class financier, regularly working with some of the largest and most successful corporations in the world. It was rumoured he was here for secret meetings with officials of unnamed governments. Caro couldn't imagine him negotiating with her. He'd be more likely to throw her out before she could do more than explain why she was here.

Then where would she be? Caro would fight with everything she had to win her daughter, but she wasn't fool enough to compare her power or negotiation skills with Jake Maynard's.

She couldn't quite stifle a choked sound of dismay.

'I don't mean straight away,' Zoe said quickly. 'Not till I've got to the bottom of the adoption process and checked some more precedents. Especially as Ariane's not in St Ancilla now. Different legal jurisdictions can complicate things.'

'As if they weren't already complicated.' Caro pushed her hair behind her ear, frowning.

'We knew that from the start,' Zoe's matter-of-fact voice cut through her troubled thoughts. She let a pause lengthen. 'Unless you don't want to proceed?'

'No!' Caro shook her head, her hair swirling again across her cheeks. She stalked to the window, pressing her palm to the cool glass. Along the horizon formidable peaks rose stark and seemingly unconquerable. Yet she knew that against the odds mountaineers had reached those impossible summits. 'I do want to proceed.' She drew a measured breath then said more evenly, 'I can't give up, Zoe. I can't.'

'Of course you can't.' Gone was the sharp voice of legal opinion, replaced by warm understanding. 'Who could, in your place?' The other woman sighed. 'Try to be patient. Time enough to talk to Ariane's guardian when I've done some more checking and we know exactly where we stand.'

As she ended the call Caro was torn between frustration and relief. Stupid to have thought there'd be any easy way through this, but after finding Ariane and spending time with her, it had felt as if anything was possible.

She'd gone to bed last night overcome by emotion at finally seeing her little girl. Being free to talk with her, watch over her as she slept. She'd assured herself it was a good sign that Jake Maynard had invited her to stay. He wouldn't do that unless she had a chance at the job.

Yet she didn't want to be a nanny. She was Ariane's *mother*.

No wonder she hadn't slept. She'd tossed all night, imagining one scenario after another where Ariane's uncle stopped her claiming her daughter.

Zoe was right. He was her uncle despite being no blood relation. Before Caro met him she'd wondered if he might be relieved to be rid of responsibility for his orphaned niece. That hope had died as she'd seen his protectiveness for Ariane.

Thinking about Jake Maynard disturbed her. He made her…unsettled.

Caro told herself it was because he had a claim to her daughter. His sharp eyes had softened when he watched Ariane. Clearly he was determined to do his best for her.

He'd never tamely give her up, even to her rightful mother.

That explained Caro's edginess. Because they were destined to be rivals, if not enemies.

It had nothing to do with the fact that he made her feel, for the first time in ages, aware of her femininity.

She couldn't be so self-destructive as to be attracted to the man who stood squarely between her and her daughter.

Caro stepped into the office, masking her nervously roiling stomach with a façade of calm. She was grateful for her father's insistence that she learn to conceal her feelings behind a show of well-bred calm. Being in the same building as her child for the first time in four and a half years tested her to the limit.

'Take a seat, Ms Rivage.'

Instead she stopped beside the desk. How could she sit while Jake Maynard paced the room?

He was even more intimidating than he'd been yesterday in his tailored business clothes. Those black jeans revealed muscled thighs and, when he moved away, a taut, rounded backside that turned her throat to sandpaper. His fine-knit pullover was a shade darker than his eyes and clung to broad shoulders and a flat belly. Even the way he'd pushed the sleeves up to reveal strong forearms dusted with dark hair did strange things to her insides.

He was potently masculine and far too disturbing.

And last night he'd called her Caro.

The knowledge beat in her bloodstream, slowing her pulse, making it ponderous with unexpected need.

For one crazy second she'd thought he might reach out to her as she grappled with yesterday's emotional onslaught. She'd been disappointed when he didn't.

When she'd thought of finding her daughter, she'd imagined Ariane's uncle as kind and ordinary. Not sucking up all the oxygen in the room. His presence shouldn't be electric, demanding, stifling the breath in her lungs.

How woefully underprepared she'd been.

He turned and surveyed her over his desk. No sympathy in his eyes now.

Not that it was sympathy she wanted.

She hurried into speech. 'I'd prefer to stand, thanks.'

One slashing eyebrow rose. 'You look like you're facing a firing squad.'

She inhaled roughly, her teeth digging into her bottom lip. How did he read her so easily?

He was right. After the way he'd quizzed her in Ariane's room last night, she knew he was suspicious of her. All through breakfast she'd been conscious of his piercing stare trained on her.

Did he hope to discomfit her? On the thought she pushed her shoulders back. He might be tough and used to taking charge but as an adversary he had nothing on her father. Jake Maynard was a hard man but he seemed to play by honest rules, unlike her devious, despised dad.

'I'm expecting to hear your decision. And after sitting for the last hour with Ariane I'm comfortable standing.'

'As you wish.' He surveyed her in a leisurely way that made her skin itch. He might have all the time in the world but she needed an answer.

He must know she was on tenterhooks. Was this some extra test to pass? Despite her joy at being in the same building as Ariane, Caro felt as if she'd been scraped too thin by the emotional overload. She hadn't slept and her mind spun relentlessly like a mouse on a wheel, trying to work out the best way to deal with this fraught, complicated situation. She didn't have answers, just the certainty that whatever she did Jake Maynard wouldn't be happy.

'You still want to work for me?'

Caro's heartbeat accelerated, hope leaping. 'You're offering me the job?' She grabbed the back of the chair.

He raised his hand. 'Not quite.' Her heart plummeted. 'To be frank I still have reservations, but,' he forestalled her when she opened her mouth to respond, 'I've noticed Ariane has taken to you and how attuned you are to her.'

That was good, surely?

'But?' She leaned forward, willing him to put her out of her misery.

His eyebrows lifted as if he wasn't used to staff demanding answers.

'But my niece's well-being comes before everything else. I want to be sure I'm making the right decision, especially as on paper you're far from the best applicant.'

Caro choked back the impulse to say Ariane could

have no better carer than her birth mother. But that would be disastrous. She couldn't reveal all too early and risk messing everything up. She had to choose her moment carefully, wait for news from Zoe. She guessed he'd resist her claim and he had far more resources at his disposal.

'So I'm offering you a job but with a six-month probationary period.' His crystalline gaze pinned her to the spot. 'If I'm satisfied with your work then we'll make it permanent.'

Permanent. That was precisely what Caro wanted.

But not permanent in the way he meant—with her as a paid carer.

Caro wanted her child. The right to love Ariane openly, to be acknowledged as her mother. Not because Jake Maynard employed her.

And, one day if she tried hard enough, maybe Ariane would love her back.

Caro's throat closed convulsively.

The situation was convoluted, with so much potential for failure. Caro met that questioning gaze. 'You accept?' One dark eyebrow slashed his brow as if he was surprised she hadn't eagerly accepted his proposal.

Caro hesitated on the brink of declaring herself. She abhorred lies yet she was deceiving this man, even if it was a lie of omission. Then she thought of Zoe's advice. And the very real possibility Jake Maynard would eject her when she revealed her identity.

So she curved her lips in the gracious smile she'd perfected almost before she could walk. 'That sounds ideal. I accept.'

'Good.'

He didn't smile. In fact, there was a crease between

his eyebrows as if something bothered him. Caro silently vowed to do whatever it took to allay his doubts.

'Ariane already calls you Caro.' He paused, her name lingering in the silence. 'I'll do the same. And you can call me Jake. There's no need for formality in front of Ariane.'

A little shimmer of pleasure exploded deep inside as Caro imagined the taste of his name on her tongue. Her pulse quickened.

A second later devastating self-knowledge slammed into her. To be thrilled at the prospect of saying his name? At hearing him say hers?

She blinked and concentrated on keeping her expression bland while inside anxiety coiled. Jake Maynard was a remarkably attractive man and she'd deliberately avoided such men for five years. Maybe that explained why he got under her skin. Whatever the reason, it wouldn't do. She had to keep her distance.

'Of course you may call me Caro.' She nodded briskly. 'However, I'd feel more comfortable calling you Mr Maynard.'

She watched his eyebrows lift, as if he were surprised to find someone who didn't instantly agree with him.

For a full ten seconds he said nothing. Finally he nodded. 'If that makes you feel better, Caro.'

Surely she imagined the way his voice dropped on her name and his intense scrutiny.

Abruptly Caro felt that, instead of blending into the background, she'd thrust herself into the limelight.

Exactly where she didn't want to be.

CHAPTER FIVE

A WEEK LATER Jake stood at his office window watching two figures track through a layer of white that was forecast to be the last, late snow of the season. They pulled a small toboggan.

When Caro had asked permission to take Ariane out he'd been sceptical. Since she'd left hospital in St Ancilla his niece hadn't shown interest in anything except staying inside with her teddy bear and toys.

He guessed her reluctance to go out stemmed from memories of the storm that left her parents dead and her trapped in their car, crushed beneath a massive tree.

Jake's belly clenched. At least Connie and Peter had died instantly.

He knew nothing about being a father, and not as much as he should about being a hands-on uncle, but he'd get there. He'd give Ariane the love and stability she needed.

Jake's mouth twisted. He wouldn't let her face what he and his sister had, a gaping hole where parental love should have been. It had been his determined older sister who'd given him the love, discipline and constancy their feckless mother hadn't.

He owed Connie everything and he was determined

to give her daughter what his sister had given him. Once this deal was through he'd ease back, spending more time with Ariane. Which meant finding a permanent home. In Australia? St Ancilla? Renting a castle in Europe was useful for his current scheme but it was hardly the home his niece needed. Nor were his high-rise apartments in Sydney, New York and London. He'd get somewhere with a garden and plenty of sunshine.

He planted his hand on the glass, watching the pair skirt the castle. Ariane wasn't smiling but nor did she look nervous, as she had previously when he'd suggested an outing.

Caro had succeeded where he'd failed.

Jake stifled what felt suspiciously like jealousy. It didn't matter *who* helped Ariane come out of her shell of grief and shock. He should be pleased.

Plus, it reinforced the fact he'd made a wise choice offering Caro the position on probation.

Yet he reserved judgement on Caro Rivage.

Because he was drawn to her?

Jake forced the notion away.

Because of her patent wariness around him?

At first he'd assumed she suffered from interview nerves but it was more than that. He felt she watched each word, each nuance, always on guard. Did she have a problem with men in general or him in particular?

Yet she wasn't scared of him. She was…cautious. And he couldn't shake the idea that she wasn't all she seemed.

Jake frowned. Should he delve deeper? Get a comprehensive investigative report?

Or was he overreacting because she kept her distance despite the way she looked at him sometimes?

As if she were fascinated, as inexplicably drawn to him as he was to her. Yet she avoided him when she could. It wasn't a response he was used to in women.

He huffed out a laugh. Was his ego so big he imagined a mystery because a woman didn't try to snare him? He should be glad. He didn't need that complication in his home.

He'd been cooped up inside too long, working on this deal. *That* was what made him stir crazy, not Caro Rivage. Maybe Ariane wasn't the only one needing fresh air.

Fifteen minutes later he approached a little valley on the far side of the castle. The air was so sharp he tasted it with every inhalation. Above was the wide blue bowl of sky and before him a cleared slope surrounded by trees.

It felt good to be outside. Especially when he heard childish giggles.

Jake's chest tightened. How long since he'd heard Ariane happy?

It unlocked memories of the last time he'd visited his sister on St Ancilla. They'd eaten outdoors under a vine-draped pergola. Connie and her husband had been the same as ever, the most content couple he knew, and little Ariane had been in high spirits, laughing at some nonsense game her father had invented with her. It had been idyllic and Jake had been glad to see Connie enjoying such happiness. She deserved it after those tough early years devoting herself to her difficult kid brother.

The sound of a husky voice interrupted his thoughts. It tickled its way through his belly then up his spine, drawing his shoulders tight.

Caro. Even if he didn't know the voice he recognised his response. The eddy of heat down low and the teasing prickle of awareness across his nape.

How was it a woman so prim and buttoned up had such a seductive voice? Last night he'd woken in a tangle of sweaty sheets, the echo of that throaty voice in his head. It had murmured an explicit invitation that made him feel as if it had been six months, not six weeks since he'd kicked Fiona out of his bed.

Scowling, he strode towards the sound.

To his surprise Ariane was on the lightweight toboggan alone, sliding down a gentle slope to where Caro waited on a broad flat area, arms wide in welcome.

It should have been his niece who captured his attention. Instead it was her nanny's amazing smile. Even from this distance it delivered a punch straight to his belly.

The sunlight on her hair picked out warm auburn highlights he hadn't noticed before. Suddenly she looked less staid and more vivacious.

She wasn't beautiful but still she was stunning. Jake frowned. It wasn't merely her hair and the colour whipped into her cheeks by the cold, but her look of sheer joy. Her smile was infectious. His mouth curled up at the corners.

Heat beat at his throat, his chest and lower. He wanted to see her smile at *him* that way instead of pretending his collar or the view past his ear was more fascinating. He wanted to see her flushed with pleasure and exertion, beaming up at *him*.

The realisation corkscrewed through him, jagging his libido and setting off alarms.

She was his *employee*. He still had reservations about her, nothing he could put his finger on but still…

'Well done,' he called out, heading towards them. 'You didn't tell me you were so good on the snow, Ariane.'

'Uncle Jake! Did you see? I slided all by myself.'

Her grin was the one he remembered from St Ancilla, from before the accident. It made his breath catch in his lungs. She'd always been a sunny child and he'd told himself she would be again. Yet seeing proof that with time and care she could recover from the recent trauma perversely reminded him again of how much they'd both lost, and how precious she was.

Nothing, he vowed, would upset her world again if he could help it.

'I saw. I'm very impressed. Was that your first time by yourself?'

She nodded so vigorously a bright coppery curl that had escaped her woolly hat danced around her face.

'Want to see me do it again?'

He nodded. 'I sure do. Then you could teach me.'

For answer she looked at Caro as if seeking permission.

The nanny nodded. 'Remember, not too high, Ariane.'

Jake watched his niece climb off and head back up the slope, dragging the lightweight toboggan behind her. He was tempted to intervene and carry her burden, or offer to accompany her but he held back, seeing the determined thrust of her small chin.

He turned to find Caro watching him, an unreadable expression in her eyes. Instantly he felt that clenching awareness low in his belly, that hot swirl in his blood.

Her arms were wrapped defensively around her middle. Did she too feel the tug between them, or was she just cold?

'I'll go and help her.' She made to turn and follow Ariane up the slight slope.

'No!' At his command she stopped, brows raised at his urgent tone. 'Let her do it herself.' Jake told himself he wasn't prompted by the need to keep the woman near him.

Caro looked over her shoulder at Ariane then nodded. 'You're right.' She slanted a look at him then away.

'What?'

She shrugged then met his stare. 'I might be wrong but I think, as well as the sheer fun of the slide, it's that sense of being in charge that she's enjoying.'

'Because everything in her life has upended?'

Caro nodded. 'All the things she could depend on have gone or changed. And though you've done what you can to establish a home and a routine, she probably feels the world is a scary place.'

The air Jake drew into his chest seemed thick and rough. She was right. Ariane had been through so much. She must feel powerless and adrift. Which was why it was important she have stability.

'You like working with her?' He hadn't consciously formed the question but suddenly he had to know. Providing the right carer for Ariane wasn't just a matter of him approving someone, but of that someone wanting to stay. Given how Ariane responded to Caro Rivage it appeared that someone was standing before him.

Caro's eyes widened. 'Of course! Why? Aren't you satisfied with—?'

Jake raised a placating hand. 'I'm satisfied. So far,' he amended. 'I wanted to hear your perspective.'

Relief drifted across her face, making her expression unusually easy to read. It was another reminder of how rarely she let down her guard with him. So she really was invested in this job. 'I love caring for Ariane. I—'

She swung her head around at the sound of the toboggan approaching, then froze. A second later she was sprinting away from him across the flat little plateau towards the steeper slope at the edge of the clearing.

Jake looked up the hill, his gut curdling.

While they'd been talking Ariane had taken the toboggan high up the slope. Far higher than the track of her previous run. Now, with the added momentum, she was skidding downhill dangerously fast and at an angle that took her in a collision course with a stand of trees.

Jake's legs were already pumping, driving him through the snow towards the far side of the clearing, even though his brain told him he'd be too late. He was too far away.

His heart sank. So was Caro. She was stumbling, trying to make headway in the snow, but, as in a nightmare, seemed to be moving in slow motion.

His ears rang when Ariane's squeal of delight turned into a cry of fear as she torpedoed towards danger. He pushed himself faster, lungs burning, but knew it was impossible he'd make it in time.

The toboggan flew towards the trees and unspeakable visions filled his head. As a one-time soldier and peacekeeper he'd witnessed terrible injuries. But this was Ariane...

At the last moment, as impact with a tree seemed inevitable, there was a blur of blue as Caro threw herself at the toboggan. Snow sprayed as it spun, there was a resounding thump and a fall of white from the branches, obscuring his vision.

As he covered the last couple of metres Jake found himself praying.

Caro lay winded, her arms wrapped tight around the small, still body.

'Ariane! Talk to me.' The deep voice was raw with fear. A fear that matched her own. For the life of her she couldn't open her eyes and face what awaited her. Had she lost her daughter again? Permanently this time?

Anguish tore at her soul.

She thought she'd known fear before but it was nothing to the terrible yawning blackness that threatened to engulf her.

All she could do was hold on, *willing* her little girl to be all right. A tightness in her chest reminded her to breathe. She drew a ragged breath that sounded like a sob. Caro should never have taken her eyes off her, not for a second.

'Ariane!' The deep voice sliced the frigid air.

Large hands covered Caro's, pried them loose. She tried to resist, opened her mouth to cry out, when a little voice said, 'Uncle Jake?'

Caro's eyes snapped wide. Above her Jake Maynard filled her vision, surrounded by cerulean sky, like an angel in a painting. Except this dark angel's face was distorted with fear and, as she watched it transform, relief. Caro felt the same emotions unfurl within, so strong nausea punched her.

Her embrace weakened as her arms turned to water. Ariane moved out of her hold.

'Are you okay, Ariane? Where does it hurt?' That resonant voice was stark with emotion.

'I don't hurt anywhere.'

Caro could swear her heart dipped and lifted on the words. Ariane was okay, she was all right.

Her own eyelids flickered shut as emotion rose like a tide, filling her chest, closing her throat, forcing her to bite her lip against the sudden, appalling urge to cry.

'Caro?' That large hand was back again, this time lingering on the pulse at her throat then skimming up to her cheek and forehead. It was hard and surprisingly callused but incredibly gentle. Who'd have thought a man with such cold eyes could have such a tender touch?

'Is she...dead, Uncle Jake?'

The fear in Ariane's voice snapped Caro out of her reverie. After what had happened to Ariane's adoptive parents her fear of death wasn't surprising.

'I'm very much alive, sweetheart.' Even if Caro's voice didn't sound like her own, far too raspy and uneven.

When she opened her eyes this time two faces peered down at her. Dazed, she took in her daughter's hopeful expression and smiled. Her skin felt stiff, as if drawn too tight, but seeing Ariane smile tentatively back was worth the effort. Her heart thudded a double beat.

Then her gaze shifted to the broad-shouldered figure beside her daughter. Had she really thought Jake Maynard's eyes cold? They flared with a heat she felt all the way to her bones. For one suspended instant everything inside her stilled then burst into flame.

'Are you injured? Can you move?' His eyes belied his terse tone.

'Give me a minute.' She drew another quick breath, pressing the heel of her hand to her sternum, trying to force her lungs into action. 'I'm just winded.' Or too euphoric to feel pain. 'You're sure you're okay, Ariane? You didn't hit your head?'

Her daughter shook her head as tears filled her bright eyes. 'I'm sorry, Caro. I didn't mean to hit you.'

As if that wasn't exactly what Caro had aimed for. Better her than a tree.

'Why did you disobey Caro and climb right up the hill?' Jake's voice was low but steely and Ariane flinched. Caro told herself it was the voice of a man reacting to fear. They were lucky Ariane had escaped serious injury.

Seeing Ariane's tears spill, Caro found the energy to sit up, curling her legs under her and pulling Ariane to her. Her daughter burrowed close, her arms creeping around Caro's neck. Caro had never experienced anything like the burst of glorious happiness that exploded inside her.

This. This was what she'd missed all these years.

For so long Caro had been tempted to fantasise that her child hadn't been stillborn. But the fantasy was too dangerous and she'd forced herself to put it aside and face reality. Then, discovering Ariane *was* alive, Caro had been so focused on tracking her down that she hadn't allowed herself to imagine this moment. It had seemed like tempting fate into stealing away her daughter again.

She rocked Ariane, breathing in the scent of snow,

pine trees and little girl. It was a perfume she'd remember for the rest of her days.

'Shh…it's okay, sweetie. No one's hurt.'

'Are you sure?' Jake Maynard frowned down at her, apparently still concerned about her. But Caro couldn't feel anything but the precious bundle in her arms.

'I'm fine.'

Ariane lifted her head. 'I won't do it again, Caro, I promise. I just wanted…' Her gaze flicked towards her uncle.

Suddenly Caro understood. 'You wanted to show Uncle Jake how well you could slide?'

Her ribs squeezed her heart. She'd seen Ariane's shy regard for the big man who was so concerned about her.

Ariane nodded. 'But I hurt you.'

'You must never do that again, Ariane,' Jake interjected, his voice gravelly. 'It's dangerous to go so high.'

Her little girl's head drooped lower and Caro rushed into speech.

'Ariane's promised never to do it again, haven't you, sweetie?' She watched her daughter's silent nod. 'And we're both okay.' Though Caro was beginning to feel an ache slide around her ribs and her shoulder throbbed. 'So why don't you show Uncle Jake how good you are at tobogganing? You could go together.'

Jake looked at her as if she'd sprouted another head and she hurried on. 'They say that if you come off a horse you should get on again straight away.' She met his stare, willing him to understand. There were enough scary things in Ariane's world without adding to them. 'I can vouch that it works.'

Caro had taken a toss off a pony as a kid and her father had insisted she get back on. It had stopped her developing a fear of horses, though they discovered later she'd fractured her wrist in the fall. She'd been more afraid of disappointing her disapproving father than of the pain.

But watching Ariane jump to her feet when Jake finally agreed there was time for *one* slide, Caro knew she was okay.

He pressed Caro again about injuries, but finally he was satisfied and she had time to gather herself, watching Jake and Ariane share the toboggan.

One slide turned into three, though at the end of each Jake strode across to check on her, his concern warming a part of her that had been frozen for a long time. Caro couldn't recall the last time any man had been genuinely concerned for her well-being. Not her father or brothers. Definitely not her ex-boyfriend who'd sold her out for personal gain.

By the time Jake announced it was time to go back, that he didn't want Caro waiting in the chill air any longer, Ariane was gleeful and her uncle's eyes had lost that stormy light.

Caro hoped that within a few days Ariane might forget how close to disaster they'd come. But her own spirits, after that initial burst of euphoria, plummeted.

It was clear Jake Maynard didn't merely feel obligated to look after his niece. He *cared* for her. And little Ariane beamed with pride and delight in his company.

What would happen when Caro claimed her daughter?

She had every right to do so. She'd been denied so much it hurt to think about the years of Ariane's life she'd missed. Even her name wasn't one Caro had chosen!

Once more she was tempted to come clean about her identity. Except Ariane was fragile and bewildered after losing her adoptive parents and Caro didn't want to add to her stress. She'd wait at least till she and Ariane had a good, strong relationship.

Plus there was another reason to delay. Jake Maynard was wealthy and powerful. If she went in assuming that because she had right on her side everything would be okay, things could go horribly wrong. Caro had been victim to the machinations of manipulative men. First Mike then her father. She'd be a fool to think Jake was any less dangerous.

He'd move heaven and earth to stop her claiming her daughter. Caro had little money of her own and her father would never support her in a court case. He'd do everything in his power to avoid scandal.

But that wasn't all. She drew a shuddering breath as she watched Jake, powerfully built and agile, utterly, fascinatingly masculine as he climbed the slope hand in hand with her daughter.

No, the worst of it was that Jake Maynard awoke something within her, a longing, that she'd never expected to experience again after years of numbness.

Desire. Not some vague sweet yearning but a piercing stab of need for his touch, his powerful body.

She sank her head in her hands. Was there any way out of this tangle?

CHAPTER SIX

JAKE COULDN'T STOP thinking about Caro Rivage. She was in his head every time he tried to read the report before him.

It wasn't figures he saw. It was Ariane's nanny, earlier today, throwing herself across the snow at risk of life and limb. Then later, limp and pale, making him curse himself for taking her word that she was uninjured.

He'd leaned down, about to lift her into his arms and carry her. For an instant he'd seen hunger in her expression. An answering beat of need had pulsed through his blood, but a second later her expression had morphed into something like fear.

Before he could prevent her she'd clambered to her feet, insisting on walking. But Jake wasn't fooled, he'd seen her stiff movements and insisted on a doctor.

Fortunately the doctor, checking out both nanny and child, had declared no harm done. Caro would suffer only bruising.

Yet Jake couldn't put her from his mind.

At least he knew he could trust her with Ariane. Caro might have been severely injured or killed with that desperate dive.

Jake's heart had been in his mouth. He wasn't used to being on the sidelines, watching others act. Guilt gouged him. He should have been the one to save Ariane but he hadn't been within reach.

The experience had changed him. Like varnish stripping away layers, there was nowhere now to hide the attraction he should *not* feel for his niece's nanny.

He tried telling himself it was because she was so good with Ariane. Even when his niece drew into herself or, very occasionally, acted up over something that to him seemed insignificant. There were times when he thought Caro too strict and others when her refusal to respond to a display of childish temper made him want to intervene. But he knew so little about child-rearing that he held back and each time he'd been glad, as Ariane became more like the engaging child he knew.

Frankly, those small displays of temper were a relief. When he'd first seen Ariane after the accident she'd been a shadow, withdrawn and wan.

Time, and Caro Rivage, were helping.

Yet hiring her hadn't been his best decision. Because no matter how he tried to distance himself, he couldn't ignore her. Or the awareness thickening his blood when she was near.

He didn't date staff.

He didn't pursue mousy women.

Yet, despite her penchant for wearing browns and dull navy, Caro Rivage wasn't mousy. The quiet manner couldn't conceal the lambent fire that blazed when she smiled at Ariane. Or when she forgot to be meek and treated him to a glimpse of that proud—and, he was sure, passionate—woman behind the mask.

That hidden woman made Jake's blood sizzle. He'd

bet every million he'd made that hers sizzled too. Today her expression had made him want to forget every reason she was off limits. To break through the tension that hummed between them like electricity through a high-voltage cable.

He'd wanted to discover if she melted at his touch.

Even the way she dragged her hair into that tight bun, like a nanny a century ago, was perversely alluring. Instead of making her look frumpy, the style drew attention to the purity of her neck and jawline, and that small but exquisite mouth. Molten heat pooled in his groin at the memory of that mouth, as pink and delicate as a rosebud.

Rosebud? Delicate?

His last lover had been confident, sophisticated and gifted with a wide, mobile mouth that she used with sinful persuasiveness. *That* was the sort of woman he dated, clever, amusing and blatantly erotic.

Why did Caro Rivage tie him in knots? The other day he'd found himself pondering her neat collarbone, glimpsed beneath the V of another primly buttoned blouse, wondering if her skin was as soft as he imagined! He'd leaned in, drawn by the hint of sweet spice in the air as she moved, till he realised what he was doing.

Jake set his jaw, shoved his chair back and shut his laptop. It was midnight but he'd never settle to sleep. He'd work off this excess energy in the gym till he was too fatigued to think of rosebud mouths, creamy skin and that husky, feminine voice.

It was a good plan. The only trouble was, when he pushed the door open to the cellar fitness complex, there was Caro standing between the pool and the hot tub, head bent as she undid the belt of her robe.

Her hair, instead of being yanked back in a bun, fell in waves past her shoulders, making her look soft and young. The guarded, self-contained nanny was gone.

Jake's throat dried as she shrugged the robe off.

She was tall, slender but with a sweet, streamlined curve to her hips. She wore grey lace-edged knickers and matching singlet top. The outfit had none of the conscious seductiveness of a scanty bikini but she radiated an innocent eroticism that dragged his libido into raging life.

Every muscle tightened as blood hurtled to his groin. Every masculine response he'd fought to control roared into life.

Attraction.

Desire.

Downright hunger.

She must have heard the door or his sharp intake of breath because she turned and he saw her eyes widen before the swell of high, perfect breasts pressed against taut fabric caught his attention. She was braless and the little jiggle of her breasts as she sucked in air drove an arrow of carnal heat straight to his groin.

Through the thickening silence came a soft sound as the robe pooled around her bare feet.

Jake's brain told him not to move even as he covered the small distance and bent to pick it up. At the same time she did.

His fingers brushed hers and he stilled. The robe fell again and he drew in a breath scented with woman and warm spice. The perfume went to his head like a draught of fine cognac downed too fast.

She straightened and he grabbed the robe from the floor, discovering it still warm from her body. His fingers curled into the towelling, rather than reach for her.

She was Ariane's nanny. His employee.

Yet he couldn't move. His soles were cemented to the floor. He was so close he saw her shiver.

Watching the flush rise from her breasts to her throat and cheeks Jake knew she wasn't cold. He forced his gaze high and kept it there.

'You're having a swim?'

Congratulations, Maynard. Full points for observation.

His thought processes grew sluggish and it was the best he could do in lieu of marching back the way he'd come. That was what he should do but for the first time he could recall, his body refused to obey his brain.

She shuffled back a half step and he wondered in surprise if she found him intimidating. This last week she'd proved she was well able to stand up to him. He saw no fear in her face. Caro wore that guarded expression he'd come to hate, because his curiosity about her had grown insatiable.

He wanted to find out what went on behind that mask of calm as much as he wanted to taste her.

Neither, he told himself, was a good idea. He dropped the robe onto a lounger and managed his own half step away. The effort made him feel as if he'd run a half marathon.

'No. Not a swim.' The husky edge to her voice was pronounced, making it burr through his belly. 'I was going to try the hot tub, if that's okay.'

'Of course it's okay. Surely Neil made it clear you could use any of the facilities.' Jake wrestled with thoughts of Caro in the hot tub. Naked? The notion locked his knees so he hadn't a hope of walking away yet.

'I...thank you, he did.' She glanced down and away as if shy. Except that didn't ring true with the woman he'd got to know in the last week. Undaunted, courageous, fiercely determined, caring of Ariane and, when it came to herself, reserved to the point of blankness, that was Caro.

Besides, though he fought to keep his eyes on her face, he hadn't missed the way her nipples pebbled against her top. The area was well heated. He guessed it wasn't a reaction to cold, especially with that telltale blush.

Reaction to him?

The idea threatened his resolve.

He should go. He'd even managed to look past her to the door to the gym when she spoke in a rush as if needing to fill the throbbing silence.

'I thought the warm water might help.'

Jake's gaze wrenched back to her then down, skating over lithe curves to the expanse of pearly skin showing between her knickers and her top. A bruise marred her pale skin on one side, the sight reminding him of her bravery today and how he'd feared for her.

'Did the doctor give you something for pain?'

She tugged her top lower and she shook her head, hair spilling around her shoulders. 'It's not that bad. I thought warm water might help me get to sleep. I feel...unsettled.'

Jake knew the feeling.

'I had a similar thought but I'm heading to the gym.'

Yet he didn't move.

* * *

Pale eyes blazed down at Caro. That silvery gaze was anything but cold. Wherever it touched her temperature soared.

Tonight, while she was suffering the after-effects of nearly losing her daughter on that snowy slope, the old, dark thoughts had circled again, waiting to swallow Caro whole. When she'd lost her baby the first time there'd been no one truly close to share her grief. Tonight she realised nothing had changed. Despite the friends she'd made in the intervening years, she was still essentially alone.

Except when she was with Jake Maynard.

The realisation slammed into her, fascinating and terrible.

With him she felt different. More alive. Less alone.

It had to be because they had a common purpose, caring for Ariane. Except as the atmosphere stretched taut around them she knew this wasn't about Ariane. It was about her as a woman and Jake as a man.

Did he feel this throb of awareness?

Caro couldn't afford to think so. Not with so much at stake. This masquerade. Ariane.

She *couldn't* risk her position here! She should run as far and fast as she could in the opposite direction.

But how could she leave when Jake looked at her that way? As if she were Venus herself, striking mortal men with yearning. A spark ignited deep inside that grew and grew as he ate her up with his eyes.

The old longing to be wanted rose again, her fatal weakness.

In childhood she'd hoped if she was good enough her family would love her. When that never happened, she'd fallen for Mike, convinced too easily of his affection. Now here she was again, craving connection.

What would it be like to be truly wanted? And by Jake, the man who occupied too many of her thoughts both waking and sleeping.

Today she'd faced the stark reality of life and death. She'd almost lost her daughter. Was lucky to be alive herself. Recklessness rose. She wanted to live in the moment.

No. No. No! Think about Ariane. The reason you're here.

She set her jaw, summoning the will to move.

'Caro.' Jake's husky whisper carved a channel through her good intentions. His hands closed around her arms, gently enough that she could have broken his hold.

Caro told herself that was what she'd do. Soon.

His head swooped down, his lips brushing hers and she lost her train of thought.

That hard mouth wasn't hard at all. It was soft, tender, impossibly tempting. Long ribbons of fire unfurled within her and she saw showers of sparks behind eyelids she hadn't realised she'd closed.

Caro drew in a breath rich with citrus, bergamot and something she'd almost forgotten, that tangy, inviting scent of healthy male flesh.

The reality of Jake touching her, kissing her with infinite care sent need shuddering through her. She swayed and reached up to steady herself. Her fingers found soft cotton, taut over hot muscle. And more, his heart thundering as fast as hers. That undid her. The knowledge he was vulnerable too.

Caro splayed her fingers over his sculpted chest and felt him shiver.

She shivered too, the ripple starting at her nape and running down her arms, her spine and right through her middle.

One second. Just a second more, then I'll be sensible.

She'd firmed her hands on his chest, ready to push away when Jake let go of her arms. Dazed, Caro registered the grinding pain of rejection and told herself it was for the best.

Except it wasn't rejection.

Jake grasped her waist. Her top had ridden up and those hard fingers spanned bare flesh. Heat drenched her. She wanted those hands on her body. Everywhere. She no longer felt self-conscious that he'd found her in drab underwear since she didn't have a swimsuit here.

All that mattered was the intoxicating warmth of his touch. His deep hum of approval vibrated through her as her mouth opened to his and their tongues embarked on a dance of mutual seduction.

The taste of him. The tenderness. The languorous sensuality. There was heat, demand, a sense of bridled ferocity as he leaned in and she bowed backwards, losing her balance, reliant on Jake to keep her from falling.

Caro's hands slipped up over wide shoulders to the back of his head, fingertips slipping into thick hair that, like his mouth, was surprisingly soft.

Now there was no thought of leaving, of doing anything more than giving in to this compulsion.

Her breathing grew short and her pulse unsteady as the kiss became more than slow seduction. She needed Jake as surely as her oxygen-starved lungs needed air.

She gloried in it all. From the feel of his muscled thighs against hers to the possessive clasp of those powerful hands and the magic of his mouth moving with hers. She shuddered as Jake's tongue swept deep in a caress that detonated explosions right through her.

When he pulled back to nip at her lower lip, then press kisses to the corner of her mouth and down to her jawline, Caro muffled a cry. He made her feel things she'd never felt before.

'Don't,' he murmured, nuzzling that sensitive spot at the base of her neck. 'I want to hear you.'

Her eyes snapped open. Eyes the colour of mercury, silvery bright, snagged hers.

'I want to know what you like.' His voice was different. Husky deep, like treacle over gravel, its rich abrasiveness turning everything inside her molten.

'Everything. I like everything.'

Caro didn't care that her voice betrayed her need. Not when he pressed close so his erection nudged her. She squirmed, planting her hands on his shoulders, trying to get closer.

'Everything?' One straight black eyebrow rose. His chest pushed her sensitised breasts as he drew a breath. Instantly her hard nipples ached and the ache drew down like an arrow, through her belly to the empty place between her legs.

She hesitated. A lifetime's practice in self-denial and caution closed her throat.

But not for long. Despite the alarm bells clanging in the back of her mind, and the hazy thought that for reasons she couldn't recall this was a bad idea, it felt so good. In Jake's arms Caro felt a wonder and a yearning that was totally new.

'Everything,' she gasped, cupping the back of his skull and tugging his mouth back to hers.

Now there was no languor, just fire and sizzling sensation. He looped an arm around her back while his other hand strayed over skin and fragile cotton, exploring, making her gasp. His fingers slid between her thighs, over her panties. She pushed up to meet his touch, eliciting a growl of approval from the mouth welded to hers.

The sound burred over her bare arms and slid like a liquid channel, down to the place where she burned for him.

Caro was aware of movement. The wide lounger behind her legs, then she was in Jake's arms, eyes popping open as he lowered her onto it and came down above her.

Fire was everywhere. Fire and longing. She plucked at his T shirt, drawing it up as she curled her ankles around his legs to stop him moving away. The press of his body set her alight.

'Wait.' It might have been an order except his voice was raw with a need that matched hers. Jake pulled back to straddle her hips, yanking his T shirt off.

Caro's mouth dried. She'd never seen a man with a body like his. Wide shoulders, a powerful, deep chest with a light fuzz of dark hair that accentuated the contours of muscles. Below that smoother skin, taut with more muscle that tapered to a narrow waist.

Caro reached for him but he caught her hands and shook his head. 'Soon.' He bent low, pushing up her old camisole top. Then he took her nipple in his mouth, drawing hard.

Caro didn't mean to cry out but the shocking delight was too exquisite. Need sang in her blood and she fought to free her wrists and reach for him.

'Patience, Caro.' He crooned her name, turning it into a caress as he moved to her other breast, using his free hand, his lips and tongue to work magic.

She felt almost overwrought at the sensations he evoked. After years of celibacy and emotional numbness, he brought her to life with a vengeance. Delight danced through her and the need for more, more, more.

When he moved lower, his tongue slicking her navel and beyond, Caro didn't know whether to weep or cheer. She loved what he was doing but she was teetering on an edge, where one nudge would make her fall off the precipice. She wanted to be with him when that happened.

Then his downward progress stopped. He traced a wide arc low across her belly. Then he looked up and the question in his eyes punctured the delirium of need.

'Caro?' For the first time since she'd known him, Jake looked hesitant. A line appeared between those dark eyebrows and his chest expanded as if on a sustaining breath. 'Are these what I think?'

Even then her bewitched brain couldn't make sense of his words. She levered herself up. He was looking at the pale striations across her abdomen.

Stretch marks.

Acquired during her eight and a quarter months of pregnancy.

Caro blinked, watching that tanned, capable hand stop on her belly. Jake's touch seemed more intimate than if he'd caressed her between the legs where she was wet for him. Sex was a finite thing, its pleasure fleeting. But carrying her child—that had changed her at the most fundamental level. It was the most precious thing yet also the source of an anguish that had haunted her for years.

She swallowed, her throat raspy and tight.

'You had a child?'

'Yes.' She didn't think of lying. She couldn't deny her daughter. Despite the masquerade she'd been forced to adopt to get close to Ariane, Caro would never do that.

It was madness to be upset now. The past was over. The future promised more than she'd dared hope for. Yet his question brought all today's emotions to the surface and pierced the armour she'd tried to build around her memories. Suddenly the past with all its terrible pain was upon her. Her guilt that she hadn't been able to keep her baby with her. She should have *known*, should have done something...

'Where is it now, Caro?'

'She.' The single word was automatic.

When the nuns had told her that her baby was dead they'd spoken of *it*, not *her*. There'd been no chance to see the child, no grave to visit, because her father had deemed it better.

Her father. He had so much to answer for. It had taken such effort even to prise out the information that she'd had a daughter.

Thinking of her lost baby as she, not it, had been a reminder that her child had been real, despite the determination of those around her to pretend she'd never existed.

Caro tried to swallow but her throat was completely clogged.

Maybe it was the gentle way Jake spoke, the concern in his eyes, now the colour of burnished pewter, dark with shadows. Maybe it was because she'd never had to answer that question before. Suddenly she felt as lost as she had years ago, both her body and her arms empty, her child taken from her.

She squeezed her eyes shut, willing the moment to pass. Trying to suppress the cold shivers.

'Where is she, Caro? Your daughter?'

It was his tenderness that undid her. She told herself it no longer mattered. She was over the grief, moving on to happier times. Yet it seemed that buried deep within was a residue of anguish that even recent events hadn't erased.

Frantically she gulped air and heard the terrible sawing sound of a woman on the edge. Past and present coalesced. Instead of seeing the little girl on the mountain who'd almost died today, it was the tiny, silent baby she'd barely glimpsed as they whipped it away. Adrenaline pulsed in Caro's bloodstream and her mouth crumpled.

'I lost her,' she whispered. 'I lost her.'

She gave up the battle and let the burning tears fall.

CHAPTER SEVEN

JAKE LAY BESIDE her and gathered Caro close, her head against his shoulder. Her tears tracking across him. His mouth set as she shook, her hiccupping breaths proof of her battle for control.

The contained, capable woman he'd begun to know disappeared. Wrapped against him she seemed fragile, slighter than when she stood up to him or when she'd kissed him. He tightened his hold.

'It's okay, Caro. Let it out.'

It didn't take an expert to know this pain had been eating away at her. Her tormented expression and the desolation in her eyes proved that. As did the fact she'd gone from the edge of rapture to blind grief in seconds. Her broken voice replayed in his ears and pity filled him.

How long had she carried this burden? Had today's drama dragged it to the surface?

Jake half rolled onto his back and pulled her across him while one hand went to the tumble of soft waves that had loosened as they kissed. He stroked her head, combing his fingers through her hair.

It was his fault she'd gone into meltdown. Why hadn't he smothered his curiosity?

But given Caro's age her baby would be young. He couldn't imagine her leaving her child in order to look after someone else's. It hadn't seemed to fit.

Now it did.

He swallowed regret, cursing his determination to uncover her secrets. Yet he was glad he knew.

Not because he was an expert in comforting distressed women. Though as a one-time peacekeeper in areas ravaged by natural disaster and violence he had some experience. But because his need to know about Caro was insatiable.

He was fascinated by her and not just because he'd doubted her suitability as Ariane's nanny.

His belly clenched as another shudder racked her. What would it be like to lose a child, one you'd carried in your body?

Jake remembered his sister Connie, her stiff upper lip as she'd told him via computer link about another miscarriage and their decision to adopt. He'd been on the other side of the world but he'd *felt* his sister's heartbreak. Jake had wanted to go to her but had been wary of interfering. The days of it being just the two of them against the world had gone. Connie had had her husband and Jake had feared intruding on their shared grief.

Who did Caro have?

There was no ring on her finger, no mention of a husband. Surely if she had a partner she wouldn't be so eager for a live-in position?

How long had she bottled up this pain?

Protectiveness engulfed him. Her abrupt transition from carnal excitement to anguish indicated she had a long way to go to come to terms with this.

Did you ever come to terms?

He hadn't given much thought to himself as a father, though over the last year he'd thought about creating a permanent base and finding a long-term partner. His experience of families and parents made him wary.

His father had abandoned them when Jake was born. As for his mother, she'd ignored her responsibilities, focusing on her own pleasure. With her stunning looks it hadn't been hard to find lovers who'd shower her with the trinkets, trips and the lifestyle she craved. That kept her away from home for weeks and months at a time till finally she found a rich aristocrat, holidaying in Australia, who wanted her long term. She'd abandoned her kids without a second thought.

Yet now he had Ariane, Jake discovered a strong streak of paternal protectiveness. It hadn't been simple, learning to accommodate a child in what had been a bachelor life. But he couldn't imagine life without her. Thinking of her rare smiles and growing trust made him glow.

If he were to lose her...

Jake rocked Caro in his arms, his lips moved against her hair as he murmured that it was all right. When, of course, it could never be all right.

Like a douche of iced water memory chilled him. The memory of Caro that first night, motionless and intent as she watched Ariane sleep. There'd been something so eerily focused about her that his sixth sense had prickled. He'd known something was wrong. Now he understood. Caro looked at Ariane but remembered her lost child.

Something plunged through his body, a weight descending to crash into his gut.

Caro's hiccups stopped and the shivers eased but she didn't move away. Instead it felt as if she was trying to burrow in his chest. Surprisingly Jake didn't mind one bit. She'd touched something inside. A chord of fellow feeling.

More. Something to do with Caro herself. He'd wondered what lay behind her façade of prim control. Now he knew at least one of her secrets. And she fascinated him more than ever.

Fascinated and attracted.

His mouth twisted. Whatever was between them, this wasn't simply sexual attraction. Sex was here— very much so, as his unsatisfied body reminded him— but so were compassion and something he didn't have a name for.

'Sorry.' Caro sniffed and rubbed her cheeks. 'I can't believe I melted down like that.' She moved her shoulders as if gathering herself to pull away. Jake's hold tightened.

'You needed to let it out.'

'Not like that. Not sobbing all over you like…' She paused and he felt the sear of her breath against his skin. It felt like a caress.

Despite everything, his body still equated Caro with sexual hunger. Jake shoved the knowledge aside, ashamed.

She lifted her head and red-rimmed eyes met his. 'I apologise. I don't know what came over me. I'm *never* emotional in public.'

Jake's eyebrows rose. 'It was hardly public.'

She shook her head and dark curls tickled him. 'It was weak and selfish to sob all over you.' She pulled back a little.

Normally the idea of a woman crying over him

would make Jake avoid her. Even now he felt discomfited by the display of such visceral emotion. He'd learned to bury emotions deep. Yet when Caro voiced the same idea, as if her grief were shameful, he wanted to reassure her.

'It's been an eventful day. Emotionally charged. Seeing Ariane in danger triggered sad memories.'

Her gaze caught his and a zap like an electric current coursed through him. Then, in a flurry of movement, Caro scrambled off the lounger. By the time he stood she was shrugging into the towelling robe, wrapping it close as if for protection.

Jake's brow knotted. Surely she didn't think she needed protecting from *him*?

But seeing the hectic colour in her cheeks, he guessed she was embarrassed.

'Caro, I—'

'Please, Jake.' She paused, the picture of discomfort.

It was the first time she'd used his name. He wished it had been in the throes of passion instead of like this. His fingers curled hard and he shoved them into his pockets.

She opened her mouth to say something, something important by the look on her face, then she shook her head. 'I need to go.'

'Stay!' He made himself stand immobile rather than reach for her. 'Have that spa. I'll leave you in privacy.' Stupid to feel rejected because she needed time alone.

Her mouth hitched at one side but it wasn't a smile. Sadness was there and a tension he supposed came from embarrassment. 'That's kind of you but I'll go to my room. I need to think.'

She hurried away, leaving him staring.

* * *

Caro had plenty of time to think but it didn't help. Whenever she made up her mind to tell Jake the truth all the reasons it was a terrible idea crowded in.

Hair damp from the shower, wrapped in her fluffy robe, she curled in the deep window seat of her turret room, her back against tapestry cushions that softened the stone wall. She hugged her knees and watched the sun rise with relief.

She'd spent sleepless hours staring at the massive peaks glimmering pale against the starry night. The view had been peaceful, at odds with the churning in her stomach. She'd wrestled with her conscience. She couldn't let Jake think her child had died. Or that she was simply a nanny.

He wasn't the cold-hearted man she'd thought. Jake was caring, not just with Ariane but with her. He'd held her and showed no impatience when her tears interrupted their passion. Her limited experience of men told her his forbearance, putting her needs ahead of his, was rare.

The gentle way he'd embraced her, the way he'd rocked her, no one had ever done that. Maybe her mother when Caro was tiny, but no one since. When she hurt she was expected to suck it up and get on with things. Even after losing her baby—no, make that having her baby snatched—she'd got little support. The nuns in the convent had seemed kind but with a distant, impersonal charity. There'd been no hugs, no shoulder to cry on.

No one like Jake.

She'd known the man a week yet in his arms, with

that deep voice murmuring reassurance, she'd felt such comfort. Such healing.

Caro drew a shuddery sigh. Her chest expanded with the first free breath she'd taken all night.

Watching dawn's rosy fingers spread across the mountains, turning indigo to peach, apricot and finally the dazzling white of snow, she made up her mind.

They all had to face the truth some time.

Today would be the day.

She'd do it one piece at a time. First the revelation that she was Ariane's mother. Then, after Jake had time to accept that, the rest. The full story would be a lot to absorb in one chunk.

Decision made, her tight shoulders dropped, the tension in her neck easing. Jake might react badly but the longer she delayed, the worse it would be.

Her relief lasted exactly fifty-five minutes. Till her phone rang while she was pinning up her hair, ready to find Jake. Few people had this number. Her lawyer, Zoe, and a couple of friends.

'Hello?'

'At last, she answers!' The terse voice splintered shards of ice down her spine. Caro froze, dropping the last hairpin. It seemed the only part of her still working was her heart, beating double quick.

'Father.'

'You remember who I am now, Carolina? That surprises me.' He thundered on. 'How dare you make me call you personally? I don't have time for this nonsense but my staff tell me you haven't answered their messages. You haven't said when you'll arrive for your brother's party. I'm forced to waste time doing the work of secretaries!'

His voice boomed so loud Caro lifted the phone from her ear. Remnants of old habits stirred. Habits of obedience and meekness. For years she'd let this man run her life and see where it had got her.

She wanted to scream that he'd stolen her child and let her spend years uselessly grieving. But she wouldn't scream, wouldn't respond to his bullying with emotion. Instead she'd be calm and in control, in contrast to his arrogant orders and malicious jibes.

When she *did* confront him it would be in person. She wanted to look him in those choleric blue eyes and let him see that he no longer had power over her. She wanted to see his reaction when the mouse of the family finally stood up to him.

'Are you there? Why aren't you answering?' Even at this distance that voice, like a thunderstorm crashing over mountains, made her skin twitch.

'I'm here, Father. And I did respond to the messages. I gave my apologies. I won't be able to attend—'

'Nonsense! Of course you'll be here.'

'Not this time.' Caro was proud of her even tone.

The silence that followed resonated with foreboding. No one, ever, said no to her father. Not her stepmother or half-brothers, not the prime minister, not anyone among St Ancilla's rich and powerful.

Caro almost wished she could see him, though the thought of being near him made her feel physically ill. Was there surprise as well as fury on that mottled face?

His voice when it came sent another polar freeze through her. 'Your brother's engagement is a major event. All the family will be there, you included.' He paused as if hearing her silent protest that she wasn't really part of the family. She hadn't been since he re-married and fathered the sons he'd so wanted.

'There'll be photos tomorrow evening before the first informal celebration. You'll be there and the rest of the week, doing your duty.'

Caro gathered her breath, storing it up in her lungs till she thought she'd burst. Her hands turned clammy and the butterflies in her stomach were the size of sea eagles.

'I'm afraid that's impossible. I—'

'I'll say this once, Carolina.' He said her name like an insult. 'It's vital we present a united front for this en-gagement. The wedding is important. Whatever you're doing in Switzerland you'll drop it immediately and come home.'

Shocked, her breath hissed in.

'Oh, yes, I know you're in Switzerland. My security staff keep me informed. I haven't asked them to dig deeper. I'm not interested. However...' he paused and the air turned heavy as if anticipating the next lightning strike '...if within the next hour my secretary doesn't receive details of your arrival time, I'll instruct secu-rity to find you and bring you home. By force if nec-essary. They're on standby. I'm told they can be with you within two hours.'

Caro opened her mouth to say kidnap was an of-fence when the line went dead.

The phone fell to her bed and she stared at it as if at a venomous snake.

Caro wrapped her arms around her ribcage where her heart thundered. She imagined the men in dark suits, driving vehicles with blacked-out windows. They gave her the creeps. They'd been the ones to spirit her back to St Ancilla when her father discovered her pregnancy, and to the isolated convent on the north of the island. They'd kept a discreet but not invisible watch on the convent and ensured she didn't run away before the baby was born.

She told herself they had no jurisdiction here. She could appeal to Jake for help. He'd protect her.

Then she imagined how that would play out. Swiss police, official reports, maybe press interest from those reporters who still kept an eye on this valley because of its connections to the rich and powerful.

Worse, she imagined Jake's reaction when he discovered not only that she was Ariane's mother, but who her family was, all in one terrible sweep. Fear pounded through her, drying her throat and churning her stomach.

She'd already decided she needed to handle this carefully. If he was bombarded with it all at once, especially with her father's henchmen battering at the door, he wouldn't take it well. He'd see her as the enemy, here to take Ariane from him any way she could. He was as likely to hand her to her father's goons as keep her from them.

Caro turned and paced, torn between distress and fury. There was something about all this she didn't understand. That final threat of her father's hadn't been simply because she'd annoyed him.

'It's vital we present a united front... The wedding is important.'

She knew enough about her father to understand he wasn't concerned about her brother's love life. It wasn't a love match but an arranged marriage. Why was her father so adamant they all be there, smiling and putting on a good show?

Caro shook her head. No time for that now. She had to figure out what to do. Unfortunately, she realised as she considered it from every angle, she didn't have a choice. Not if she wanted a chance to discuss Ariane's future calmly with Jake without her father interfering.

Jake strode the corridor towards his office. It was early but after a night of little sleep he might as well start work. The consortium he was trying to entice into this project was proving difficult to pin down. He needed to concentrate on that rather than Caro.

The woman perplexed him, intrigued and attracted him. He couldn't recall responding to any woman like this. Not even Fiona, his ex-lover, the woman he'd fleetingly considered as a possible spouse.

Every time he thought he had Caro pegged she surprised him. She awakened a host of unexpected feelings.

He turned a corner and slammed to a halt. There, silhouetted against the window, was Caro near the door to his office.

Jake recalled the feel of her slender body curving into his, the baffling intensity of the emotions she'd evoked and the less puzzling arousal. Then she'd worn next to nothing. Now she was in one of her drab skirt and jacket sets, in a colour that reminded him of mud. And still excitement throbbed in his blood.

She stared at a painting on the wall, the early sunlight limning her profile. Jake told himself she wasn't stunning the way some of his lovers had been, yet there was something about that pure profile, the angle of her chin, the neat curve of her ear and that long slender neck that drew his eye.

She moved and he caught a glint of russet in her brown hair. It reminded him of the fire that ignited in his belly last night. And of the volatile, passionate woman who'd turned to flame when he'd kissed and caressed her.

Heat punched low. All night he'd struggled against the need to go to her room.

To check if she was okay, he reasoned.

To take up where they'd left off, he knew.

Only the depth of her hurt had stopped him.

Caro swung around. Had she heard the sudden heft of his breath? Her eyes widened.

It was back, that pulsing heat. She bit her lip and he absorbed the fact she looked nervous, no, more than that. Scared. She swivelled back to the painting, fingers plaiting restlessly before her.

Her fear made him hesitate. She *couldn't* be scared of him.

'You like it?' Jake asked as he neared, forcing himself to look at the picture. He'd barely paid any attention to it. In the flood of morning light he discovered the face of a sombre man holding a globe and surrounded by maps and papers.

Caro shrugged and he noticed the movement was stiff, as if her shoulders were too tight.

Was she self-conscious after last night? He couldn't blame her, yet he wanted to make her turn and look at him.

'It's…interesting. At least four hundred years old.' She spoke quickly as if to fill the silence. As if nervous.

'I can't work out what it's doing here, in the direct sunlight. It should be in a protected position.'

'Maybe it's a copy.' Jake knew little about art and, though the castle's owner had provided an inventory, he hadn't looked at it. He was here to work, and build a relationship with Ariane, not stare at paintings.

Caro shook her head. 'Unlikely.' She bent closer. 'Highly unlikely.'

'You know old paintings?' If he'd been watching the portrait instead of her he would have missed her flinch.

'I studied art history.' She darted a sideways glance that didn't meet his eyes.

'I don't remember that on your résumé.'

She lifted one shoulder. 'I didn't finish and it didn't seem relevant.'

True, but Jake wanted to know more. Much more.

'It's my fault about the painting.' At his words she swung to face him. Jake felt that familiar tug low in his belly when their eyes met. As if someone dragged a weight through his insides. 'It looked gloomy so I had it moved out of my study.'

'I see.' For a moment longer their eyes held, then her gaze slewed back to the painting and Jake found himself cursing her discomfort with him. He preferred her passionate and bold.

And eager for sex.

Heat spiralled like smoke up from his groin and he had to work at keeping his distance. Clearly she was nervous.

'I think you should move it.' Another darting glance. 'It shouldn't be here in the full sun.'

'I'll get Neil onto it.' He paused, watching the tic of

her pulse at her throat and the way her hands refused to be still. 'Caro, we need to—'

'I have to—'

Both pulled up short. 'You first,' he invited.

Caro nodded but didn't look eager. 'In your office?'

'Sure.' He pushed open his study door and invited her to precede him. As she walked past he caught a hint of her warm, spicy scent and it went straight to his head. For a second he closed his eyes.

He'd be good. He wouldn't seduce the nanny in his office.

No matter how much he wanted to.

Caro's fingers twisted together, echoing the churning inside. This was more difficult than she'd thought.

She'd half hoped she could blame last night and the way she'd thrown herself at Jake on the high-octane mix of fear and elation resulting from Ariane's near accident. But it was still there, the desire for his touch, the yearning for his tenderness and passion.

Worse, she wanted to blurt out everything, ignoring the need to approach this carefully.

Hurriedly she looked down, veiling her eyes from that sharp scrutiny.

Her heart hammered and no matter how she tried she couldn't pull off the mask of composure she'd come to rely on. Because she wasn't just fighting her attraction to Ariane's uncle. Now her father had thrust his oar into these turbulent waters she felt in danger of being tugged under by forces too strong to withstand.

Now, instead of telling Jake the truth and trusting he was truly a decent man with Ariane's best interests at heart, she was forced to lie again. Because she couldn't afford to risk him withdrawing and taking her daughter away.

She felt sick.

'Caro?' A firm hand closed around her elbow. 'You look like you're going to keel over. Here.' He ushered her to a chair. 'Sit.'

She subsided thankfully, even as she castigated herself for weakness. This wasn't how she'd meant to face him. But when she'd seen him, all her hard-won resolve had disintegrated. She'd jabbered on about art instead of cutting to the point.

'Thank you. Sorry, I'm fine. I…' She shook her head. 'Something has come up. I need to go away for the rest of the week. I know it's not usual and I should give you notice but it's urgent.'

'Away?' His eyebrows tilted down. In curiosity or annoyance?

'To St Ancilla. I had a call from my…father this morning.' She couldn't suppress the shiver down her spine.

'Bad news?'

'A family matter. I'm needed there.' She paused and licked dry lips. 'Normally I'd never dream of asking for time off so soon but I don't have a choice.' Her father had seen to that. Caro straightened. 'I'd be back next week.'

Finally she looked him square in the face. What Jake saw there made everything inside him still. Not just tension but distress, and that fear he'd picked up on in the corridor. He'd read it as embarrassment after last night's intimacy. Clearly it was caused by something far deeper.

Not everything revolves around you, Maynard.

'Your family needs you.'

'I know it's inconvenient and I apologise but—'

He stopped her with a wave of his hand. Clearly this was important. From her expression he guessed serious illness or accident.

'Of course you can go.' What wouldn't he have given for the chance to spend even a few extra minutes with Connie, instead of being informed from the far side of the world that his sister was dead? 'Take what time you need. Lotte and I will manage.'

For a second her lip wobbled then she nodded briskly. 'I'll be back next week. You can count on me.'

CHAPTER EIGHT

'Jake, did you say it was St Ancilla Caro went to?'

Reluctantly Jake looked up from his emails. This project grew more complex by the hour and he wasn't devoting as much time to it as he should. He'd spent the morning with Ariane.

On the other hand, his niece's ease with him felt like victory. He owed her thawing, in part, to Caro, who'd done an amazing job in a short time. He'd been right to hire her.

Neil sank into the chair on the other side of his desk. His expression was unreadable, yet the fine hairs on the back of Jake's neck stood to attention.

'That's right. What's happened?'

Jake leaned back in his chair. A tough early life, a stint in the army then years devoted to wheeling and dealing in the turbulent field of international finance meant it took a lot to unnerve him.

'I tracked down another on our list of potential investors and discovered they were in St Ancilla for a big event.' Neil passed his tablet across the desk. It displayed a news article. If you could call it real news. Some royal event.

'So? Wait a few days then make contact.'

'Check out the photo. The second one.'

Jake looked again, scrolling past a photo of a young, formally dressed couple smiling at the camera with all the animation of marionettes. Prince Paul of St Ancilla and Princess Eva of Tarentia, just engaged.

Beneath was a group photo. An ornate balcony on an imposing building, crammed with elegant women and men in heavily decorated dress uniforms.

'And?' Jake had no interest in aristocracy. He did business with them but his personal experiences with them hadn't been happy. First had been the entitled foreigner who'd lured his mother away, on condition she abandon her kids. Then just months ago, his own girlfriend suggested he put Ariane in an orphanage rather than bother with her. Both had been uncaring of anyone else, expecting the world to revolve around them.

'Look closely. The one in blue.'

Jake frowned. Several of those uniforms were blue, plus a blonde in ice blue and...

He stared. It couldn't be.

Of course it couldn't. The woman in the deep blue dress was a vibrant redhead, not a brunette. Yet Jake felt adrenaline burst into his blood with a jolt.

He zoomed in on the woman, amazed at the likeness.

'Princess Carolina of St Ancilla. The King's eldest child.' Neil's voice was flat with suppressed excitement.

'*Princess* Carolina?' Carolina. Caro.

No. It was impossible. Mere coincidence.

Yet the buzz in Jake's bloodstream didn't abate.

'Yes, but she's not his heir. Her younger brother is. Carolina isn't in the limelight these days. She lives fairly quietly in the north of the island though she's very active in a number of charities, especially relating to children.'

Jake peered at the woman. She was a ringer for Caro, except for the clothes and hair. And the royal connections.

'Maybe our Caro is a distant relative.'

Our Caro? His choice of words made her sound—

'There's more.' Neil took the device and opened another page, handing it back. With his usual efficiency he'd collated a precis on the woman.

The Princess had a string of names, had been born almost twenty-five years ago and lost her mother early. Her father had remarried when she was two and she had three half-brothers. She'd studied in the US but didn't finish her degree. There'd been a scandal. He read headlines about wild parties and drug use. Jake wasn't surprised. Most of Fiona's privileged friends preferred parties to work. What did surprise him was that after returning to St Ancilla, Princess Carolina had all but dropped off the radar. She didn't live in the palace, merely appearing in the press at charity events or major royal celebrations like this, her half-brother's engagement.

He scrolled lower, studying the shots Neil had collected. Stiff and formal on the same balcony with her family when she was a little girl. Again in her teens, looking almost gawky despite her expensive clothes and with her flame-coloured hair now turning auburn, her head turned towards her father, her expression curiously closed. A shot of her with one of her brothers, both smiling for the camera but neither looking happy.

Jake began to feel almost sorry for her. Had the wild partying been rebellion after an unhappy childhood?

Then he scrolled lower and his breath caught.

This photo was different. Candid. He doubted she knew it had been taken. She wore casual clothes, her hair in a ponytail and she was in a crowd with other young people. At a party, by the look of it. She was half turned away, looking over her shoulder, but there was no mistaking the warmth in her expression as she smiled at someone beyond the camera. Her eyes, a remarkable deep violet, glowed. *She* glowed. Jake felt the impact of her joy judder through him.

He swallowed, mesmerised by those eyes. They were so like Ariane's that for a moment everything, his pulse and his breathing, seemed to stop. He'd always thought the colour rare. Maybe not so on St Ancilla.

He touched the screen, enlarged the photo and then his breath really did stop.

There, on the back of her shoulder next to the strap of her top, was a small birthmark shaped like a comma.

Jake had seen that mark three nights ago.

It had peeked out beneath the strap of a grey camisole when he'd held Caro in his arms.

By midnight the scowl on Jake's face threatened to take up permanent residence. His emotions veered between shock—he who'd believed nothing had the power to surprise him any more—fury and grim determination.

There was pain too, a sliver of hurt that he'd allowed her to play him as she had, but he buried that deep.

There was no time for such luxuries. With every hour came a new revelation. That was what happened when you could afford the best investigators.

No wonder the initial check of her application hadn't found any criminal record for Caro Rivage. She didn't exist, except technically, for Rivage was the family's name though royalty traditionally didn't use it.

Caro was royal. Daughter of a king. Her full name and titles took up four lines on the report filling his computer screen.

Jake stared at it and felt the blood jump in his arteries as if seeking a way out. His body was screwed so tight even an hour with a punching bag had done nothing to relieve it.

Once they knew which direction to pursue, the investigators hadn't taken long to prove Princess Carolina and Caro Rivage were the same person.

Some of what she'd said was even true. She had worked in a preschool. The references had checked out because she'd actually worked as a nanny for a couple of families. In between swanning off in couture clothes to charity events and royal parties. That in itself was curious. From socialite royal to nanny wasn't a normal progression. But she was definitely royal.

There was a photo of her taken six months ago at a ball, wearing a tiara and a complacent smile that made him grind his teeth. A tall guy with medals across his chest and a hungry expression was at her side, holding her as if he didn't want to let her out of his sight.

Jake swore and shoved his chair back, stalking the length of the room. He understood the feeling. The woman couldn't be trusted an inch.

Yet still he registered that hum of expectation deep inside. The expectation of what would happen when he held her in his arms again. Even her bald-faced deceit hadn't destroyed his desire for her.

He ploughed his fingers through his hair and spun on his heel, pacing again.

She'd lied from the first. Not only about her identity. About everything.

That scene by the spa? Had she waited for him, knowing he often worked out at night? She'd sucked him in with her passion and counterfeit distress. First reel him in by giving him a taste of what he wanted, a taste of mind-blowing sex, then play on his protective instincts to stop things going further. She'd teased and distracted him.

Ego told him she *had* been attracted to him. He'd seen the evidence almost from the first.

His brain said it was all a lie. Or if it wasn't, even if she had wanted him, she'd wanted something more, to lure him into feeling sorry for her. She'd wanted him in the palm of her soft little hands.

That sob story about needing to go to her family? The implication, unspoken but there in every throbbing silence, that some terrible tragedy had occurred? All lies.

She'd gone to a *party*!

Was the tall guy with the possessive look there with her? Or had she moved on to some other gullible bloke?

Jake frowned as pain radiated up his arm. He looked down and saw he'd pounded his fist against the stone wall beside the bookshelves. Gingerly he unfurled his fingers, feeling pain slice through his hand and seeing a graze of blood.

The woman had got under his skin in ways he could barely believe.

Even Fiona hadn't made him so furious. Because he'd begun to see her true colours despite her efforts to paper over the cracks of her innately selfish personality.

With Caro... Carolina, he'd been completely taken in. Except for that tingle of premonition that she wasn't what she'd seemed. He'd been distracted by his need to find a way to connect with his niece, and his attraction for a charlatan.

She hadn't just lied about her identity. If only that were the worst of it!

He shoved his hands in his pockets, peering out at moon-washed peaks, taking in the twinkle of lights further down the valley that made him feel, for the first time in years, as isolated as he'd been as a kid, shutting himself off in an attempt to lessen the pain of his mother's desertion.

He'd actually *felt* for Caro. Had wanted to care for her as much as he'd wanted her in his bed.

Whereas she didn't want him. She wanted Ariane.

Nausea swirled in his belly and he swallowed the rancid taste of disgust.

If the investigators were right, Ariane's birth mother was Princess Carolina of St Ancilla. Everything pointed to it. The way she'd been bundled home when news broke of her wild partying. Her seclusion at a convent on the northern end of the island for the better part of a year. The fact that Ariane's adoption took place in the same region and there appeared to be a link to the same convent.

As if that weren't enough, someone else had been investigating Ariane's adoption lately, requesting records and asking questions. A lawyer in St Ancilla. A lawyer related to the countess who'd supplied a reference for her friend, the masquerading Princess.

It was easy to see what was happening. A group of aristocratic friends colluding to help each other.

Why?

The answer made Jake's blood steam.

So the pampered Princess could get her hands on Ariane.

Jake shook his head, breathing deep and filling his lungs as far as they'd go. Even so it felt as if barbed wire wrapped around his chest, constricting his air, drawing tighter as his ire rose.

He didn't give a damn if some party-girl princess had a change of heart about the baby she'd abandoned. Ariane was better off without her. For what was to stop her changing her mind again?

What Ariane needed was love and stability. Family. That was where he came in. *He* was family.

Carolina of St Ancilla signed away her rights years ago. It was too late to change her mind. Ariane was his niece, his only link with his beloved sister.

He had no intention of giving her up to some spoiled, deceitful woman who used her body to get her own way.

A shudder stormed his frame as he thought of her giving herself to man after man, a commodity to get what she wanted. She was an expert cheat, given the way she'd fooled him. An expert at using sex and deception.

But she'd messed up this time.

He'd never release Ariane to such a woman.

He might have been born working class and only just avoided being made a ward of the state when his older sister stepped in to raise him. But he was a man to be reckoned with. Apart from his considerable wealth, he had powerful contacts.

More, forewarned was forearmed. He wouldn't wait till the Princess tried to snatch Ariane, or filed a lawsuit to claim her.

Right now arrangements were being made to increase security on the castle and on Ariane in particular. No one would steal her away.

As for a lawsuit… His mouth curled disdainfully. He already had a team of the best legal experts onto it. Birth mother or not, Carolina wouldn't get custody. If he had his way she wouldn't get access to Ariane for years. By which time her whim to be a mother would no doubt have passed.

Jake's smile became a grin. He wanted to see her face when she discovered she'd been outmanoeuvred.

Caro's smile felt like a rictus and her fingers ached from shaking hands with the throng of people her father had invited to the ball. Yet a glance at the mirror on the other side of the palace foyer reassured her. Her smile appeared real and she looked as regal as jewels, haute couture and years of mind-numbing training in etiquette and deportment could make her.

Her father would have nothing to complain about tonight, at least as far as she was concerned. No doubt he'd find something else to take umbrage at. He was never happy unless unhappy with something.

What had possessed him to invite such a huge crowd? Not only royals and people from both St Ancilla and Tarentia, but a slew of others. There was an unusually high number of foreign bankers and financiers.

Surely the whisper she'd heard couldn't be true—that the royal finances were rocky.

Caro pushed the idea aside. Probably her father planned some new scheme and had decided to finance it with someone else's money.

She smiled at another guest, answering him in his native German, hiding a wince at his too hearty handshake.

Through the formal welcomes her mind kept straying to Ariane. Was she sleeping or was she beset by the nightmares?

Did she miss Caro?

Caro told herself it was too soon for that, though *she* missed her daughter with a permanent ache beneath her ribs. After years believing her child dead, the impatience to be with her grew stronger not less. She'd only just resisted calling again tonight to check on her. Lotte had been reassuring this morning when she phoned. That had to be enough.

Soon she'd be free to go back to the castle. To Ariane.

And Jake.

Sinuous heat swirled through Caro's middle at the thought of Jake.

Feminine desire battled with trepidation whenever she thought of him. The man she'd almost given herself to. The man she wanted. She, who'd believed no man could ever again tempt her into intimacy, much less trust.

The man who'd been considerate and caring in a way unmatched by any other man in her life.

The man who stood between her and her daughter.

Except surely the person she'd seen behind the forbidding exterior and rapier-sharp mind needn't be an enemy? He wanted the best for Ariane. Surely, once he knew the truth he'd understand. Cooperate.

Caro clung to that thought through the last of the welcomes. In a couple of days she could return to Switzerland, see Ariane and explain to Jake.

He'd be surprised at first but he was no ogre. They'd find a way to negotiate this situation and—

'Princess Carolina.' The deep voice, like trailing velvet dipped in arsenic, wrapped around her.

Her thoughts shattered. Slowly, using every effort to turn a neck suddenly stiff with tension, she looked to the next guest.

She felt herself sway, wondered distantly whether she might black out. But she didn't have the luxury of escape.

Jake Maynard stood there, superb in formal clothes tailored lovingly to his tall, broad-shouldered form. He'd looked daunting in business clothes, vital and handsome in a knitted pullover and jeans, raffishly sexy in gym gear. It shouldn't surprise her that in a bow tie and dinner jacket he was devastating.

Yet he stole her words as well as her breath. Caro stared up at the man watching her with the hooded silvery gaze of a predator. So handsome, with such a palpable aura of danger and power she instantly thought of a fallen angel. Or maybe that was because of the hot mercury stare pinning her to the spot.

'Or do you prefer to be called Caro?'

Nearby someone snatched a shocked breath at his effrontery but Caro was too busy standing tall when that poison-drenched voice wound tight around her, stopping the air in her lungs.

Without waiting for an answer he captured her hand. Instead of shaking it, he lifted it slowly, ostentatiously. He didn't bend his head, instead raising her arm high so she could see her pale hand in his as he pressed his lips to her fingers.

Involuntarily her fingers curled around his as energy jagged from her hand up her arm and down to her breasts and lower, to that empty space deep inside. The blood racketed around her body so fast she felt light-headed.

Caro heard a hissed breath, hers, then felt the convulsive shiver of her body's response. To him. To the anger sizzling in that half-lidded stare. And, heaven help her, to his bold challenge.

'Mr… Maynard.' Her hesitation made it sound as if she was trying to remember his name, which was better than revealing how undone she was as he stood there, arrogantly stopping the queue of guests and holding her hand so close she felt the warmth of his breath on her fingers. The flesh across the back of her shoulders drew tight and her skin prickled. 'How good of you to attend.'

'You were expecting me?' His eyebrows rose as if in polite enquiry but Caro was busy reading the rest of his face. The grooves carved down his cheeks by the tight set of his jaw, the pronounced tic of a pulse at his temple and the flare of his nostrils as if assailed by some unpleasant smell.

Caro wavered on the verge of panic. She couldn't do this. Not here, not now. She needed quiet, a place to explain away from curious ears. She needed his understanding and compassion, not his enmity.

But finally Caro steadied herself. She had no option.

'I hadn't realised you were on the guest list but I hope you enjoy the ball.'

'I'm sure it will be most entertaining.' Still he didn't release her hand. She was conscious of the increasing number of stares trained on them.

'Please go on through.' She nodded towards the double doors flung wide to the gilded ballroom. Footmen stood on either side of the entry with trays of champagne. Beyond them guests milled, quaffing drinks, showing off their finery, chattering in anticipation.

Slowly he lowered her hand. But instead of releasing it, Jake curled his fingers around hers. His hold tightened into an implacable grip that matched the forbidding angle of his jaw. 'Perhaps you'd like to show me around, Your Highness?'

The suggestion defied royal protocol and good manners. She was here with her family to greet their guests.

'I'm sorry.' She made to pull her hand free but found it trapped. 'But I—'

'An excellent idea,' the familiar voice boomed from nearby.

Caro's face jerked around to find her father, resplendent in a scarlet uniform almost a perfect match for his colouring, beaming at them. Beaming! Her father!

Caro had a powerful moment of disbelief. So strong she wondered for a second if she'd strayed into a dream. Even her stepmother beside him wore a slight smile.

'You two young people go ahead. Enjoy yourselves. We're almost finished here.'

Inadvertently Caro caught the eye of a long-term diplomat in the queue, waiting to be greeted. In his eyes she saw a reflection of her own astonishment.

Her father was a stickler for the rules, especially those promoting formality at court.

'Thank you, Your Majesty.' Jake inclined his head then, before Caro had time to catch her breath, he led her smoothly towards the ballroom.

As they stepped into the glittering room with its ornate ceiling paintings, crystal chandeliers and scores of massive mirrors, his breath whispered across her cheek.

'I'm sure tonight will be memorable.'

He spoke softly but the look in his eyes, and the feel of those long fingers manacling her wrist, sent a chill of deep foreboding straight to her marrow.

CHAPTER NINE

JAKE WAS KNOWN for his self-control. For an early responder in disaster zones it had been a quality almost as important as his skills at organisation and saving lives.

Yet tonight sorely tested him.

She tested him. Waltzing by on the arm of the man who'd held her possessively in that photo.

The simmering heat in Jake's gut rose in a seething flood of impatience. His plans to confront her in a quiet anteroom had been foiled by the press of people, all wanting to speak to her or him. Then there was the sheer formality of the proceedings. Her first dance had already been allocated and, short of hauling her away in front of a fascinated audience, he'd had no choice but to relinquish her.

He gritted his teeth, berating himself for the spurt of fury that had propelled him to the palace. He should have waited and chosen his venue better but his blood was up and for the first time in years he'd acted rashly. Goaded by the smiling redhead in the dark violet dress.

Simply watching her did excruciating things to his self-control. Jake told himself it was wrath but there was an edge to his anger that felt like more.

Like want.

Worse, like disappointment, because he'd felt something for her.

Except the person he'd begun to know was a mirage, constructed by the duplicitous woman now swanning around the dance floor. Her long skirt belled around her legs, calling attention to that tiny waist and acres of creamy skin bared by a dress that hung off both shoulders.

Jake's blood pounded in counterpoint to the beat of the waltz. Colours blurred and faces flashed by but still he had no difficulty keeping her in focus. Caro Rivage aka Princess Carolina. She moved with a grace that despite his anger evoked raw hunger in the pit of his belly. Or maybe it was the smile she gave her partner, bending to murmur in her ear.

They swept past and for a second violet eyes caught Jake's. Wide, impossibly beautiful and, if he didn't know better, scared.

No, this woman wasn't scared. Disconcerted perhaps but she'd brazened it out, introducing him to guests as if they really were simply acquaintances. Keeping up a flow of small talk that made him want to muffle her mouth with his till she was so breathless, speech was beyond her.

With difficulty Jake slowed his breathing, searching for calm. They needed to talk. He needed confirmation of what he'd learned. Needed her to admit it. Then he'd inform her she had no hope of getting Ariane.

Sanity resurfaced. He told himself to wait till tomorrow when he could see her alone.

Except that would give her time to regroup. He'd find her surrounded by lawyers and royal officials who'd try to deflect him. This was between the pair of them. He wasn't in the mood to wait.

The music ended and her skirts spilled onto the gleaming floor as she curtseyed to her bowing partner. He was Prince of Tarentia, Jake had learned. Brother to the woman whose betrothal they were celebrating. How cosy. No doubt the two royal families were close. Maybe there was a second wedding in the pipeline?

Jake grimaced as acid stirred in his gut. Caro inhabited a privileged world where old family connections mattered and worth was measured by inherited wealth and titles.

But her privileged past didn't give her the right to sail into Ariane's life and disrupt it. To make the little girl believe her birth mother cared, only to be crushed when she discovered the woman who'd borne her had no staying power.

Jake knew how that felt.

He wouldn't let it happen to Ariane.

Stalking forward, he cut through the milling crowd to Caro and her partner.

'My dance, I believe.'

He didn't wait for a response, ignored a protest from the Prince and slipped his arm around Caro's waist. As he claimed her he felt her jolt of response. Satisfaction stirred. A second later the music started and Jake propelled her into the centre of the dance floor.

He hadn't planned to dance, had decided merely to separate her from her partner, but this was the simplest way to do it.

It had nothing to do with the greedy way his fingers splayed over her narrow back. The surge of rampant triumph as he pulled her close. The way her eyes dilated and that glossy cupid's bow mouth opened as if she couldn't catch her breath. Or the sheer rightness of her slender form in his embrace.

She matched his steps as if they'd danced together before. As their bodies had aligned perfectly when they'd kissed and when he'd held her, sobbing in his arms.

Jake tasted disgust on his tongue. Those tears had been faked. *She* was fake.

He glanced at the fine golden wires studded with purple gems threading her auburn hair, the matching long earrings that swung with her every move. Heard the swish of her rich ball gown billowing around his legs. But the trappings of royalty meant nothing to him. Glamour couldn't make up for a good heart. The fact his body still responded to her only made him more determined to wrest himself and his niece free of her pernicious influence.

'So tell me, Princess Carolina. Since you're the eldest in the family, why aren't you married yet? No desire for a family and children of your own?'

Caro faltered and would have tripped but for Jake's iron-hard embrace. He didn't slow at her misstep, swinging her, if anything, faster into the next turn, so she had to clutch him to keep her balance. Hard muscle and warm fabric teased her palms.

The mention of children hit her like a blow to the solar plexus, the impact shooting through her body and turning her legs nerveless.

For a heartbeat, for two, she could do nothing but hang on and try to keep up.

She shouldn't be surprised he was such a superb

dancer, he had the strength and agility of an athlete. Yet it was his words, not his moves that worried her.

How much did he know? Her double identity, certainly. Anger radiated from him in waves. But not, surely, the rest, about being Ariane's mother.

'No plans to settle down with your Prince Charming?' He didn't bother keeping his voice down and the glittering challenge in those icy eyes told her he relished the idea of her objecting and trying to quiet him. No doubt he'd say something more outrageous.

Was that why he was here? To embarrass her?

For several seconds her tongue stuck to the roof of her mouth. A lifetime's reserve, of doing as she was ordered and being the one to back down, urged her to murmur something placatory. She hated scenes.

The twisting distress in her belly urged her to flee.

Caro did neither. She looked him straight in the eye.

'No plans to marry, Jake.' She pronounced his name casually as if they were old friends. As if the taste of it on her tongue didn't evoke a clandestine thrill of self-destructive pleasure. 'And you? Are you looking for a wife? I could introduce you to some lovely women here.'

She let her gaze drift over the crowd as if searching for said women. As if she weren't avoiding his blistering contempt.

For years she'd caved at the first sign of her father's displeasure. Even now she was nervous about the prospect of facing the King when she finally got time alone with him. But for some reason, standing up to Jake, despite the knowledge he stood between her and Ariane, made her blood sing in her veins.

'I've no intention of marrying.' The words bit like

glacial shards, grazing her skin. 'I have too much experience of lying, manipulative women to trust one that much.'

It was a direct body blow. Caro felt it smash through skin and bone, felt herself absorb it like soft flesh cushioning a knife thrust.

It didn't help that he was right. She *had* to lied to him. But how could she have done otherwise? She'd had her reasons, as he'd discover when she had a chance to explain.

'You need to be careful. You sound like a misogynist. You don't want to turn into a lonely old grouch.'

A flash of something that might have been astonishment lit his features then disappeared. His lips rucked up at one side in a derisory smile that perversely reminded her of how wonderful his mouth had felt on hers a few nights ago.

'No danger of that, Caro. There are always women chasing me. Some even smuggle themselves into my life undercover.' Her breath caught at the steely light in his eyes. 'But I can tell a woman on the make. They don't have a hope of getting what they want, no matter what inducements they offer.'

His gaze dropped slowly, insolently, to her mouth, then lower, to her throat, bare of jewels, then across her décolletage. Suddenly the beautiful dress she wore seemed totally inadequate to protect her from that scorching, lazy stare.

Indignation rose, fiery and glorious, eclipsing nerves and her innate dislike of scenes.

Abruptly, after months, no, years, of coping and carrying on despite the hurt, Caro reached breaking point.

She was tired of being wrong-footed. Of being assessed by men and found wanting. By her father, who'd ignored and belittled her because she wasn't a boy. By Mike, who'd read her gullibility then turned nasty when he discovered she wasn't the docile meal ticket he'd assumed. He'd taken cruel delight in telling her she was far below the standard of his usual lovers.

Now by Jake Maynard, who made her feel cheap. Because in a moment's madness she'd dared to act on the attraction shimmering between them.

It hurt. All her life those rejections had hurt.

She'd had enough.

With a strength that surprised her, Caro wrenched free of his hold and stepped back. She saw his eyes widen then she swung away through the swaying couples.

There'd be speculation and shocked looks but she didn't care. She marched on till she was out on the terrace, lit by flambeaux and still too full of people.

Behind her she heard something that might have been her name but it was drowned by the beat of blood in her ears. Turning, she headed inside again and down a corridor, the sound of her high heels clicking on inlaid marble matching the quick thud of her pulse.

Still she continued, past state rooms, dining rooms, libraries and offices, past startled footmen bringing supplies from the kitchens.

Her ball gown swung wide as she turned up a familiar staircase, skirts lifted for speed, her breath coming in raw gasps that betrayed her pain.

Along another corridor, right to the end of the palace furthest from the rest of the family's rooms. There, highlighted on a wall, was the victorious knight in armour, running a lance through a whimpering dragon.

Caro didn't have to look to know the knight wore the same look of cold disdain Jake had as he'd stripped her soul bare.

Caro pressed a hand to her pounding heart and wrenched open the door to her rooms.

Sanctuary at last! At least for the ten minutes she'd give herself to regroup.

She swept in and turned to close the door but a dark figure loomed in the doorway. Before she could react Jake inserted himself into the closing gap, crossed the threshold then stood, looming over her.

'Perfect,' he purred in a deep rumble that danced along her bones. 'Just what we need, a quiet place to continue our discussion uninterrupted.'

Fingers welded to the doorknob, Caro struggled for breath. His effrontery left her speechless.

'No! I want you to leave.'

'Why? Are you scared to be alone with me? You'd rather have witnesses for this discussion?'

'It's not that.' Despite his anger she wasn't scared of Jake Maynard. More of her inability to deal with him until she had her emotions under control. With him she felt as if she walked a tightrope, one false move and she'd fall into…she wasn't sure what, but every sense screamed she couldn't go there. Especially with so much at stake.

Caro drew herself up, projecting the regal assurance the rest of her family did so well and for which she'd had to struggle.

'I didn't invite you here.' The sight of that big, brooding form in her private sanctuary sent a strange jolt through her. As if he trespassed on something more fundamental, more personal than a mere room.

'That's unfortunate, *Princess* Carolina.' He said her title as if it were tainted. 'We have so much to talk about.'

Caro hefted a breath that didn't fill her lungs and tried to get a grip. 'We do. But not here. Not now—'

Jake shook his head. '*Yes*, here and now. And as for you not inviting me, let me be absolutely clear.' He bent towards her, thrusting his starkly sculpted face into her space. 'I would never have invited you into my home if I'd known who you were. You owe me.'

Caro's eyes bulged at the venom in his voice. 'Look, I know my identity is a surprise and I regret not telling you in the beginning but I had excellent reasons—'

'To lie and cheat? Perhaps to steal too?' His eyebrows contracted in a mighty scowl and the atmosphere thickened as if a thunderstorm threatened.

'I don't cheat and I definitely don't steal!' Horror mixed with an anger she couldn't suppress, despite the voice inside telling her she needed to be calm and reasonable. That had always been her default position.

And look where it got you!

'So you say. But from where I stand you're a liar and a cheat.' He shook his head. 'To think I almost felt sorry for you with your sob story the other night.'

'I wasn't lying!' Her distress had been only too real.

'Except your baby didn't die, did it, Caro?' He stepped so close his breath wafted warm across her skin. 'Your child is alive and well.'

'You know?'

How did he know? It didn't seem possible. She'd never have believed it herself if she hadn't finally been told the truth by someone who'd been there. The knowledge staggered her. Her numb fingers slid from the doorknob and Jake shut the door with a solid thud, closing them together in the shadowy room.

'I know.' There was no satisfaction in his eyes, only a burning emotion she felt like a brand on her skin. 'And I tell you now, you can't have her. You'll *never* have her. I'll do whatever is needed to make sure of it.'

'No!' She wasn't aware of launching herself at him but suddenly she was grabbing his lapels, leaning into him as if she could change his mind by the force of her desperation. 'Don't say that.'

His big body froze, all except for the rise of that wide chest and the quick flick of the pulse at his temple.

'Are you going to try using your body again to persuade me? It won't work this time.'

'I'd *never* do that!'

'No?' He looked so supercilious, staring down at her with hateful superiority. It dragged up memories of the many times she'd felt powerless, when others, principally her royal father, had twisted circumstances against her. 'You're saying you had no ulterior motives when you offered yourself to me? You weren't using your body to get what you want?'

Caro didn't want to think about what had happened that night by the spa, much less try to explain her actions. Not to this grim-faced stranger who bore only a superficial resemblance to the Jake Maynard she'd come to know.

That man was gone, if he'd ever existed outside her imagination.

Yet to Caro's dismay even his piercing disapproval didn't eradicate her profound response to him. Furious as she was, her body still registered the excitingly hard outline of his solid chest, the breadth of his shoulders that made her feel appallingly aware of her own feminine desires. A crazy part of her actually revelled in this flashpoint of physical intimacy though they were on opposing sides.

'Don't be insulting. I'd never do that.'

'No? Because you're a virtuous, responsible royal princess who never put a foot wrong?' Jake shook his head, his eyes not leaving hers, his tone censorious.

'Because you'd never make the headlines for drug use and drunkenness, would you? Or have an illegitimate child and abandon it and the father without a second glance?' Impossibly his expression hardened even more. 'Did you *once* think about where your child might end up? Leaving a vulnerable baby to the mercy of total strangers because you couldn't bother facing your responsibilities?'

Caro would have staggered back in horror except Jake wrapped a powerful arm around her waist, holding her against him.

'You don't deserve to be a mother.' His voice hit a low note that resonated through her bones. It reminded her of the terrible, insidious voice of despair that had hounded her darkest days after the loss of her baby. 'You might have been born with a silver spoon in your mouth but you're nothing but a selfish sl—'

The slap cut his words off, rocking his head to one side.

Pain burst across her palm and up her arm. Belatedly he captured her hand, pressing it against his shoulder. She saw his jaw work and the bloom of dull red across his cheek.

'You don't shut me up so easily, *Princess*. I'm not

one of your lackeys, afraid to offend royalty. I tell it as I see it and as I see it you—'

Caro couldn't listen. Nerves stretched to breaking point, body shaking from the desperate surge of adrenaline filling her blood, she did the only thing she could think of to stem the flow of vitriol.

Rising on her toes, she smashed her mouth against his.

CHAPTER TEN

A THUNDERBOLT SHEARED through Jake, cementing his feet to the floor. His body rocked, hands clasping her tight.

As if he feared she'd step back?

Impossible.

She was a liar, a cheat. He couldn't trust a word that came out of that beautiful deceitful mouth.

Yet as Caro's lips sealed his and her soft breasts pushed against him something shuddered through him that wasn't abhorrence or repudiation.

Desire. Hunger.

Need.

A need so powerful it made a mockery of the diatribe that he'd spewed out. Even her resemblance to his faithless mother, abandoning her children because they didn't fit her chosen lifestyle, faded into the background.

In his arms he held fire and feminine passion. A desperation that matched his. She tunnelled her free hand through the hair at the back of his scalp, pulling his face down as she kissed him with an urgency that sent every sense throbbing into overload.

Already clinging to the borderline of control, Jake

opened to her kiss, letting her tongue slip between his lips. He reciprocated, devouring her mouth with a thoroughness that spoke of this woman's seductive allure as much as his own recent celibacy.

Somehow this physical attraction survived disillusionment. Incredibly, it wasn't eclipsed by negative feelings. Fury and desire coalesced into something headier, stronger, hotter than he'd ever experienced.

He wanted to despise himself, wanted to wrench away from her pliant body and the addictive sweetness of her mouth. Yet he couldn't.

She gave a mew of satisfaction that coiled through his vitals. He realised he'd bent her back over his arm, kissing her the way he'd like to take her body, with a single-minded carnality that already had him fully erect.

Jake tried to gather the ragged remains of his self-control. This was the second time she'd kissed him, each time trying to play him for a sucker.

Yet even that knowledge couldn't quell his need. It was bone-deep, undeniable and, it seemed, unquenchable.

The only way out was to make her pull back.

He covered her breast, warm and thrusting towards him. His grasp tightened and he heard again that encouraging purr in the back of her throat.

Jake told himself he was spurred by the need to make Caro retreat. He hooked his fingers into the top of the strapless dress and yanked. Impossibly soft flesh pillowed the backs of his fingers. He yanked again and the purple dress came down just enough to reveal a creamy, raspberry-tipped breast, not large but an exact fit for his hand.

Jake's erection throbbed as he covered her with his hand. Instantly an electric current zapped up his arm, lifting the hairs on his nape before shooting down, straight to his groin.

Caro watched him beneath drowsy eyelids. But there was nothing passive about that purple-blue stare. Jake felt the air freeze in his lungs as their gazes meshed.

Deliberately, driven by a compulsion he couldn't resist, he bent, kissing her nipple then drawing it into his mouth.

The assault on his senses was instantaneous. The delicious taste of her. The flood of rich, feminine scent, delicate yet sensuous in his nostrils. The incredible surge of arousal.

Far from repudiating him, Caro arched higher, lifting her pelvis to bring her lower body flush against him, cushioning his erection against soft flesh.

Fumbling, Jake hauled down more material, exposing her other breast. He worked it with his hand, the other with his mouth, and the sound of Caro's faltering cry of pleasure drove him to more lavish caresses.

His groin was iron hard, forged and furnace hot.

For an instant, no more, he retained enough sense to hesitate, then caution shattered and he gave up the fight.

He wanted Caro so desperately his hands shook. The taste of her drove him wild. The sound of her panting, the hitch of her breath when he suckled harder, were pure encouragement.

So aroused it hurt to move, he straightened, pulling her upright and ignoring her pout of disappointment. With kiss-swollen lips and bare breasts pushed up towards him by the dislodged bodice, she looked like some raunchy male fantasy come to life. The contrast of all that exquisite bare flesh with the prim tiara still nestled in her bright hair made him feel as if he were debauching Cinderella.

Except those eyes, that mouth, held erotic awareness.

For this moment it didn't matter what she'd done or planned to do.

Who knew that fury and physical desire could be such potent bedfellows? That hate sex could be so powerful?

'Sorry?' He'd seen her lips move but his tumultuous pulse drowned the words.

'I said, don't you dare stop.'

Satisfaction crested like a curling wave thundering down onto a beach. Finally he had the real Caro. Stripped of lies and subterfuge. As vulnerable as he to the stark force of mutual attraction.

Ridiculously Jake's heart lifted. They both wanted this, both needed it. And when it was done the niggling ache he'd felt ever since Caro Rivage stepped into his world would be gone.

He couldn't wait.

Sliding his hands down warm silk to that slender waist, he lifted her off the ground, intending to find the bedroom. But the movement brought her exquisite, jiggling breasts high. His mouth dried, his ability to plan more than a few steps ahead disintegrated and instead he deposited her on a nearby piece of furniture. He didn't know what it was, only that its height meant she now sat almost level with his groin.

Without hesitation he stepped closer, hands in her voluminous skirts. Caro didn't try to stop him. Her knees fell open, inviting him closer, and her own hands were busy tugging his bow tie undone, ripping at his shirt.

Finally his questing hands met sheer nylon. He closed his eyes in frustration. He should have guessed a princess would wear pantyhose for a ball. He'd have to—

His fingers touched bare flesh. Stockings, not pantyhose. Elation rose. He touched lace between her legs, then, sliding his fingers beneath it, damp curls.

A shudder of lust racked Jake. He set his jaw, searching for the willpower to exhibit some control.

Soft hands palmed his chest, nudging his shirt and jacket wide. They slid down from chest to navel, to the top of his trousers. A second later nimble fingers undid his trousers.

His eyes snapped open as his clothes fell away and her hands curled around his length.

Arousal quaked through him. His skin pulled taut as heat shot hard and heavy to his groin.

Jake pulled her against him, his lips on hers, driving into her welcoming mouth.

There was no thought involved as he bent his knees to bring his erection to that sweet spot between her thighs. Or tugged her lacy underwear aside. Only the same instinct that made him plant one hand on her hip, tilting her towards him.

Something stirred in his brain. Some thought he couldn't catch. Something…

She shifted and suddenly he was there, the head of his shaft testing slick velvety heat. Her tongue swirled against his, her hand tightened on his length and the fragment of thought disintegrated.

Pulling her hand away, he planted it on his backside before drawing her legs over his hips and plunging into her beckoning depths.

Someone groaned. Was it him?

Caro's fingers wrapped possessively around his neck while she laid waste to his senses with that eager mouth. Her other hand clawed at his glute as if to hold him exactly where he was.

But Jake couldn't stay still. With a deliberate slowness that took him right to the edge of sensory overload, he withdrew then thrust again, deep and sure. Instantly she quivered. Tiny ripples of movement that coalesced into a powerful, clenching shudder that drew tight around him and hurled him over the edge with her. It was too soon, far too soon, but he was powerless to resist the force of this rocketing climax.

He was no stranger to sexual gratification but this pleasure was so sharp, so intense he lost himself utterly.

Instead of darkness there was light and colour. The deep blue-purple of the sky at twilight surrounded him, drugged him, lulled him through the force of that potent climax until, a lifetime later, it resolved into Caro's wide eyes, holding his in dazed wonder.

Jake shivered as aftershocks powered through him and he spilled again and again in hot, urgent pulses.

Even when it was over he couldn't process anything like a clear thought. Only the need to stay where he was, lodged within her, eaten up by those big violet eyes, with her long legs wrapped tight around his hips and his soul in paradise.

Finally, tentatively, he shifted his weight, only to feel her hands clutch tighter as if she couldn't bear the separation.

He understood the feeling. They hovered in a cushioned cloud of ecstasy.

Yet as the thought rose, so did others. Jake remembered the sheer perfection of losing himself in her intimate heat, pulsing hard and unfettered.

Because he hadn't used a condom.

The realisation cramped his gut and foreboding feathered his spine.

Jake closed his eyes, silently cursing his loss of control. It had never happened before and he'd believed it never would. How had it happened? Because Caro Rivage was a sexy siren who drove men out of their minds?

He breathed deep, inhaling the smell of sex and woman. To his amazement, despite the shock of his dangerous behaviour, Jake found it arousing.

Was this how she'd got pregnant with Ariane? Driving some poor sod crazy with desire so he forgot to take basic precautions?

No. Jake wasn't such a poor excuse for a man. He'd acted of his own volition. It had been his responsibility as much as Caro's to think about safe sex. He'd failed. For the first time in his life he'd let his libido conquer common sense. He despised himself for that.

Drawing a deep breath, he withdrew, clenching his teeth and shutting his eyes at the tormenting friction against sensitive skin.

If he wasn't careful he'd be ready to go another round with her and make exactly the same mistake. Even now he was tempted to forget everything but the need to bury himself in Caro's lush body and take them both to heaven again.

Which was why his movements were quick as he

yanked up his underwear and trousers. He didn't trust his control when they were skin on skin.

Control? He grimaced. He had none around this woman.

The sooner he put a distance between them, the better. Sex with the enemy was a mistake. One she'd hope to exploit in her favour. Best he set her straight immediately. Jake opened his eyes and his mouth at the same time but what he saw stopped the scathing words he was trying to form.

Instead he cursed under his breath.

For Princess Carolina hadn't moved. She sat, tiara at a tipsy angle in that dark red hair, cheeks hectic with a blush that spilled all the way down her throat and covered her trembling breasts. Her hands were clamped, white knuckled, to the edge of the carved wood where she perched and her shoulders bowed forward as if in defeat.

Despite the temptation of those perfect breasts, it was her expression that compelled his attention. Lines of pain gathered around her mouth and furrowed her forehead. Worse, glittering tear tracks spilled down both cheeks.

He'd hurt her.

She'd conned him and led him on. But he'd hurt her, and the sight of her pain made him feel wrong inside.

Caro closed her eyes, just for a second. *Then* she'd be strong. Then she'd pick herself up and face what had to be faced as she'd always done. Because there was no alternative. She was alone, always had been, with no champion but herself. She didn't have the luxury of weakness.

But when she'd seen Jake grimace...

There'd been no mistaking his disgust, the shudder of distaste as he pulled away. Disgust at what he'd done. Disgust at *her*. Because she'd lied and because he'd given in to the raging need for sexual completion that had sprung up between them like a clawing beast.

There'd been nothing civilised about their coupling. It had been raw and intense, fulfilling a primitive need that was beyond her limited experience. Sex with her ex-boyfriend had been pleasant but not compulsive. Caro didn't understand the desperate woman who'd invited, gloried in being shoved onto an antique chest and taken without finesse or preamble.

It didn't matter. What mattered was that Caro had loved it. Had exulted in being ravished with such urgent thoroughness, eager for Jake in that visceral way as if she'd waited for him her entire life.

It had been glorious. *He'd* been glorious and made her feel special, strong, *wonderful*.

Until he realised what he'd done and hated himself. As he hated her. He'd stuffed himself back into his trousers so fast she guessed he feared she might touch him again. As if her touch tainted.

She recalled the ugly words he'd shot at her like bullets from a gun.

A great shudder built behind Caro's ribs in the vicinity of her heart. It curled round to her spine then up to her skull and down to her pelvis. Finally, mastering herself, she swallowed, put her shoulders back and forced her eyes open.

To find a grey gaze surveying her with what looked like concern. Something skimmed her cheek. She jumped then realised it was Jake's hand.

Caro leaned back. She should pull up her bodice, she realised as she registered her unfettered breasts and the discomfort of the boned bodice pushing them high. But her hands were too unsteady. Besides, he wasn't looking at her bare breasts but her face.

'You're crying.'

'Rubbish.' She turned her head away and began to wrestle with her dress when gentle fingers brushed her cheek again and she felt the smear of wetness there.

Caro stilled. Blinked.

Horror slammed into her. Bad enough to see his distaste, but to have him witness her distress was mortifying. This was the second time she'd cried in front of him. She, who'd spent years burying her emotions!

'I was rough. I hurt you.' Jake's voice sounded different, not the familiar mellow rumble that tickled her insides but taut and scratchy.

'You didn't hurt me.' Caro looked down, focusing on the bodice she couldn't tug up. Probably because she was sitting on the dress, holding it down. Desperately she shifted her weight, trying to drag the skirt higher so the bodice would move.

'Then why are you crying?'

'I'm not!' The tears must have escaped earlier.

Instead of moving away, Jake confounded her by capturing her chin in his broad palm and lifting it so she had to look him in the face.

'You looked like you were in pain.'

Of course she did. No woman wanted to be abhorred. But Caro couldn't bring herself to say that. The pain was still there but she masked it as she'd learned to mask so much.

'You're wrong. I'm fine.'

Except for the anguish deep inside. And the other, disturbing sensation that urged her to lean into his touch and ask for more, as if she had no pride.

Those pale eyes were intent. 'If you weren't in pain, why did you cry?'

Caro shrugged. 'It was an intense experience. It surprised me.'

She waited for him to say something offhand or derogatory. Instead she thought she saw a glimmer of understanding in his face. Until his next words.

'Not because we had unsafe sex?'

It was like being smacked in the face. Her head reared back in disbelief. She gave up struggling with her dress and wrapped her arms protectively around her chest, as if to ward off his words. But, pressing her thighs together, feeling the wetness, she realised it was true.

How could she not have given it a thought? With Mike she'd been the one to insist on safe sex, despite his protests. It had been like fate laughing at her to discover she was pregnant, given the precautions they'd taken.

Her eyes locked with Jake's and she read her surprise reflected back. And more. Something that again, fleetingly, looked like understanding.

'I'm safe,' he said. 'You won't get any health problems from me.'

Except a possible pregnancy.

Caro bit her lips rather than blurt the words. Her first accidental pregnancy showed she was, or had been, very fertile. Her mind boggled at the idea of another baby. Jake's.

His forehead creased as watched her. 'This is where you're supposed to say you're clean too.'

'I'm clean too.'

'You don't sound very convincing.'

Probably because she was still stuck on the possibility of pregnancy. If it could happen once…

'How many lovers have you had lately?'

Caro frowned, his terse tone penetrating the fog of shock. 'None.' Then, when he lifted his eyebrows in disbelief, 'Well, one, but years ago. When I got pregnant.'

For long moments nothing moved except her blood pumping and the unsteady rise of her chest with a new breath. Jake looked as if he'd been turned into a statue. A frowning, disbelieving statue.

'You're telling me you've only had one lover?' At least his voice wasn't starkly accusing, but his disbelief tore at her self-respect.

She hiked her chin higher, profoundly glad that her crossed arms covered her bare breasts.

'Is that a crime? I don't ask how many you've had. I take your word that you're…clean.' She was lucky she was too, given what she'd discovered about Mike's lifestyle.

'What about the wild parties that made the headlines? The drugs and sex that made your father bring you home?'

Cold shivered through Caro. 'You know about that? You really are super-efficient, aren't you?'

Jake's shoulders lifted. 'I employ Neil for his efficiency.'

Nausea curdled her insides. She thought she might actually be ill. Bad enough that Jake, who despised her, thought the worst. Somehow the idea of Neil, the quiet, funny man who had treated her with such kindness, believing the press reports made her feel like vomiting.

'It wasn't true,' she said finally, her strangled voice not her own.

'Sorry?'

Anger rose and she was glad. Anything was better than feeling defeated and miserable. Caro stiffened her spine and met his gaze proudly. 'The stories weren't true. My boyfriend, Mike, was the one who partied to excess and took drugs, though I didn't know about the drugs till later.'

'How very convenient.' His mouth curled and suddenly Caro had had enough.

Ignoring the need to cover herself she put both hands to his chest and pushed. He was physically stronger but eventually he stepped back, leaving her free to slide off the high chest onto her feet. Caro gritted her teeth, her clammy hands slippery on the silk as she tried to right her dress. But the bodice refused to rise.

'Let me.' A big hand covered her shoulder, turning her. Before she knew it he'd lowered the zip of her dress.

'Stop that! I don't want—'

'Try again now that the dress is loose.'

He was right. She hadn't been thinking clearly. Of course it was easier without the bodice tight around her middle. This time the material rose easily and she sighed in relief.

A second later the zip rose and with it the touch of Jake's fingers on her back. Fire sizzled from there, loosening her spine and her resolve. Did she imagine his touch lingered then slid into a caress?

Setting her jaw, Caro stepped away, almost crying out at the loss of his touch. It made no sense. His distaste should have cured her of any attraction yet to her shame she still longed for Jake Maynard.

'It's time we talked.' To her surprise his tone had lost that harsh, hurtful edge.

She glanced at the time, realising in horror that they'd been away from the ball longer than she'd imagined.

'I should go back.'

Then she caught their reflection in the mirror on the far wall. Jake looked stern but attractive, the only sign of their carnal interlude his sexily rumpled hair and missing bow tie. Already he'd done up his shirt.

She, on the other hand, looked utterly...wanton. Her lips were swollen, her hair a mess and her designer dress suggestively crushed.

'If you show up looking like that you'll create a scandal.' He might have read her mind.

'If I go back wearing something else it will be just as bad.' She lifted a hand to the tiara listing to one side. She wanted to take it off but it was secured with scores of pins and her fingers shook.

Caro was damned no matter what she did.

'Father will be livid.'

To her surprise the thought, instead of making her feel worse, lifted her spirits. She hadn't set out to cause a scandal at her brother's party. From Paul's expression since she'd returned to St Ancilla he had too much on his mind to worry about gossip. His would be an arranged marriage but Caro suspected it wasn't a happy arrangement. However, the idea of annoying her father, childish as it was, pleased her. She still hadn't had the opportunity to confront him alone about stealing her baby.

Caro swung around to Jake Maynard. The man who'd once been so warm and kind. The man who'd been so cruel that remembering his words slashed at her soul. The man who was her enemy. And her lover.

The man she wished would sweep her up in his arms and take her back to that rapturous place she'd known for such a short time. At least now he wasn't sniping at her. He was ready to listen.

'You're right.' She felt the weight slide from her shoulders. 'It's time I told you everything.'

CHAPTER ELEVEN

SHE SWITCHED ON a lamp and its mellow light turned her into a mediaeval illumination with her rich auburn hair, violet-blue eyes and deep purple gown.

Jake sat on an armchair opposite and reminded himself not to trust her. Just because she made his pulse hammer with longing, because her mix of defiance and melancholy twisted him inside out, didn't mean he could relax his guard.

Yet it was hard to reconcile the woman who'd clung to him as if he were her whole world with the scheming liar he knew her to be.

He ignored the treacherous urge to sit with her on the sofa. This time he'd think with his head, not another part of his body.

'How did you change your hair, your eyes?' It wasn't the most important question but he still wasn't accustomed to her flagrantly exquisite colouring.

She looked like a painting by an old master brought to life. Except the memory of her toned, surprisingly strong body was vivid. This woman was no delicate work of art. She was bold and so alive his skin tingled being close to her.

Because you still want her. Despite everything.

Their eyes locked. Jake's pulse thudded.

'Coloured contacts and a rinse. I visited a hairdresser in St Ancilla to get me back to my natural hair colour for this week. The rinse wouldn't have lasted anyway and that would have given me away. But I was impatient to see Ariane.' Her mouth crinkled in a moue of self-derision. 'When I finally discovered where she was I couldn't wait. I acted rashly, but I had to see her as soon as possible.'

She shrugged and Jake was surprised at how the simple movement of bare shoulders could so entice. He jerked his gaze back to her face but Caro wasn't looking at him. Her eyes were fixed in the distance.

'What was the plan? To snatch her?'

Now Caro looked at him, her face full of astonishment. An act?

'I'd never do anything like that. Apart from anything else, Ariane just lost the only parents she knew.' Did he imagine her voice wobbled on the word 'parents'? 'She's struggling to cope with the changes in her life. Kidnapping her...' Caro shook her head, staring as if *he* were the one at fault. 'She needs stability, not more trauma.'

Caro drew a deep breath. He watched as she sat straighter, chin up, hands loose in her lap. With the movement she became more regal, more untouchable. He fought the urge to go over there and reduce her to the desperate lover she'd been minutes ago. Sexual awareness still thickened the atmosphere and his body was taut and eager.

'I acted on impulse applying for the job. My lawyer advised me to wait before confronting you. And

I thought if I told you the truth you wouldn't let me see her.'

Jake's hackles rose. There, she finally admitted it.

'You plan to claim Ariane.' Bitterness filled his mouth.

'She's my daughter.'

Caro spoke quietly but with a pride Jake couldn't mistake. Nor did he miss the sparkle in her eyes.

Just as well he'd taken the precaution of increasing his niece's security. He hadn't brought her to St Ancilla. He didn't trust this woman's royal relations not to twist the law in their own country and rip Ariane from him.

He shook his head. 'You gave up your rights to her when you abandoned her.'

Despite her wounded look he didn't hide his disdain. He abhorred mothers who deserted their children.

'Let's get one thing straight.' Jake leaned forward, his hands fisted on his knees. 'You're not Ariane's mother. My sister was. She and her husband were the ones who sat up with her through the night as a baby. Who suffered the sleepless nights. Who played with her and loved her and taught her everything she knows. *Not* you. It never *will* be you. Not while I've got breath in my body.'

Jake's words were arrows, piercing her heart. Reminders of all she'd missed. All she hadn't been able to give her daughter.

Would Ariane ever forgive her for that?

Caro swallowed convulsively, ignoring the blistering pain as the acid of his hatred penetrated. How could she have given herself to a man who despised her?

Yet even on opposing sides, Caro felt that trembling awareness that was always present around Jake. Shame engulfed her. Even now she couldn't conquer her yearning.

'It wasn't like that. I didn't abandon her.' Caro drew a shuddering breath. 'She was taken from me.'

Jake lifted his eyebrows in disbelief.

Finally he spoke. 'They still believe in fairy tales here? You'll have to do better than that, Princess Carolina.' She hated the sneering way he said her name. 'No one could take your child unless you wanted it gone. You were an adult, a mother. You had responsibilities. So did your lover. Yet you both gave her up.'

His words echoed the guilt that dogged her in the darkest hours. The shame, the belief that somehow she should have intuited the truth and stopped them taking her baby.

Caro blinked, feeling the hot glaze at the backs of her eyes but refusing to shed more tears.

'Ariane's father died before she was born.'

Jake stilled, a frown descending. Then he shook his head. 'You're after sympathy?'

'No!' She looked down at her hands, twisting in her lap. 'All I want is for you to hear me out.' She'd hoped to skate over some details but Jake already knew so much and had put the worst interpretation on those. She had to make him understand. 'Can you do that?'

For answer he crossed his ankles and leaned back in his seat, his silvery gaze fixed on her like a steely skewer.

For all his sprawling arrogance Caro had the crazy urge to get up and kiss him full on the lips till he lost that haughty attitude and scooped her close. Because,

bizarre to admit it, she'd found not just carnal satisfaction with him but something more. Something that
had, for a fleeting time, felt strong and real and good.

How many times could she fool herself into believing what she wanted to believe? Surely Mike had cured
her of that.

Shifting her gaze to the small landscape painting on
the wall beyond Jake, Caro cleared her throat. 'After
school I was allowed to study in the USA. It was the
first time I'd lived outside the palace.'

'And you kicked over the traces, of course.'

Her gaze slewed back to his. 'There's no of course
about it. I was nervous but excited. To have the free-
dom to make my own friends, not the ones approved
by my father...' Looking at Jake's stony face, she gave
up trying to explain.

'I spent a lot of my time studying. Art history
mainly. I'd hoped eventually to work in a gallery or
museum.' That dream was long gone. She frowned,
dragging herself back to the point. 'When I was there I
met Mike, another student. He was everything I wasn't.
Confident, outgoing, charming—'

'You do yourself a disservice.' Jake's drawl interrupted her. 'You were all those things at the ball tonight.'

Her eyes darted to his then away. 'Learned skills.
In Mike it was innate. He was...' She shrugged. 'Actually, he wasn't the man I thought he was. But I fell for
him. We became lovers and I was as happy as I'd ever
been.' The change had been amazing after her dour
family situation with her perpetually disapproving father and a stepmother who saw her as an encumbrance.

'We did go to parties and some of them got out

of hand, but I usually left early. I wasn't into drugs.'
Which was why she hadn't realised the signs that Mike
was. She'd truly been naïve. 'Then I found out I was
pregnant. I suspect Mike tampered with the condoms.'

'Another bit of embroidery, Caro? Young guys aren't
generally eager for parenthood.'

'Mike wasn't like most guys. I discovered later that
he saw me as a ticket to wealth and privilege. Getting me pregnant was his insurance policy.' She met
Jake's narrowed eyes and hurried on. 'At first it was
so romantic. He proposed and I accepted. I thought we
were in love and we'd have a wonderful future. Until I
came home early one day to find him in bed with another woman.'

Jake leaned closer, his disbelief replaced by anger.
He muttered something savage that, though it couldn't
change the past, made Caro feel better.

'I was devastated.' Looking back now, she'd had a
lucky escape. Cold iced her bones as she imagined not
discovering Mike's true colours till after the wedding.
She rubbed her hands up her arms.

'I dumped him and when I refused to take him back
he turned nasty. He wouldn't give up. His moods became erratic, possibly because of the drugs he was
taking.' Caro shivered, remembering how he'd frightened her.

'He threatened you?' Jake's gaze darkened.

'It doesn't matter now. What matters is that he contacted the palace. He told my father I was pregnant,
hoping my father would force me into marriage. He's
very strict and wouldn't abide me bringing up an illegitimate child.' Caro grimaced, remembering.

'But you didn't marry.'

'No. My father paid him for his silence.'

So much for the undying love Mike had professed. Even after all this time that had the power to wound. All her life she'd longed for love. She had only the vaguest recollection of her mother's warmth. 'With Mike's help the press got hold of stories of me partying wildly. My father used that to explain my return to St Ancilla.'

'And your lover?'

Caro tilted her head, surveying Jake. Why the curiosity when he knew Mike was dead?

'He used the money to indulge himself. He died of an overdose months after I left.'

'I see.' Jake scowled and Caro wondered what it was he saw. 'So you came back here, to your family.'

Her mouth twisted in a smile that held no humour. 'Not to the palace. Nor to my *family*.' She drew a sustaining breath, remembering how frightening it had been, hustled from the airport by a team of anonymous men who wouldn't even speak to her, much less tell her where she was going. 'I was taken from a private airport to a convent on the other end of the island. I was kept on the estate there till after the birth. My only contact with my family was a note from my father saying he'd see me after my little problem was resolved.'

'And you agreed.' Was Jake's anger directed at her or her father? Suddenly tired, Caro didn't care.

'Of course not. I walked out several times. When that didn't work I tried to sneak away. I didn't get far. His security team had the place under surveillance and they were very...efficient.' Even now the sight of her father's minders made her feel sick in the stomach. 'I had no phone or computer and my friends didn't know where I was. My father said nothing but I discovered later that *"sources close to the royal family"* hinted I was recuperating from an unspecified health condition.'

Caro saw the flash of confirmation in Jake's expression and knew he'd read those rumours that she'd been in rehab or recovering from a breakdown.

Sitting, recounting those days was too much. She got to her feet and paced to the window, clutching the curtain as she looked across the royal gardens, lit with thousands of lights for tonight's party. Her father would be furious at the scandal she'd caused. Already gossip would be in full swing.

But now the prospect of his temper didn't make her cringe. She wouldn't give in to his bullying any longer now she had something to fight for. Ariane.

'I gave birth there.' It was easier speaking about it with her back to Jake. Despite her father's wishes, Caro had resolved to raise her baby, even if it meant leaving St Ancilla with nothing. But she'd underestimated her father and her weakness after the birth.

'It was long and difficult.' She'd lost a lot of blood and drifted in and out of consciousness. 'I never heard the baby cry. I didn't see her, just the midwife's back, taking her away. They told me she was stillborn.'

Caro swallowed and unlocked her stiff fingers from their death grip on the curtain. She pressed her hands to her stomach, remembering the terrible anguish of that night, fighting the urge to bow her shoulders and curl in on herself.

She focused on the garden illumination and the strains of music in the distance.

'It took a while to recover. Afterwards I refused to

return here, except for official events. I made my home at the far end of the island, working with children.' Caro cleared her throat, striving for a lighter tone. No need to explain that after losing her baby, she'd been driven to connect with other children.

'Recently I was contacted by the younger of the two midwives who'd been at the birth. She'd just had her first child and...' Caro faltered then made herself continue. 'She said she'd always felt guilty about what happened that night. But it was only when her daughter was born that she knew she had to tell me the truth. She said my baby was alive. That it was taken away, she assumed for adoption.'

Caro forced down the tangle of distress choking her throat.

She'd have to do better than this when she confronted her father. The knowledge gave her the energy to turn and look at Jake.

To her surprise he was no longer sitting, but stood mere paces away, on the other side of the window. His expression was unreadable yet he radiated tension. It hummed from him, making the hairs on her arms stand up.

'You know the rest.'

His hooded gaze raked her. 'I have the resources to check your story.'

Because even now he didn't believe her? The knowledge sent adrenaline buzzing through her, as if she'd taken a shot of spirits. A laugh emerged from her dry mouth. 'Is that a warning? Go ahead. The more corroborating evidence, the stronger my claim to Ariane.'

It was the wrong thing to say. That half-lidded stare

turned laser bright and, despite her resolve, trepidation scuttered down her backbone.

But Caro was done with giving in to bossy men. She wanted her daughter and no one was going to stop her. She met Jake's narrowed eyes with determination.

Jake gritted his teeth, refusing to argue. Time, and the best investigators and lawyers, would give him the ammunition he needed. No matter what had happened in the past, Ariane was his niece and she needed him. He'd protect her with his life.

Yet Caro Rivage muddied the waters with her story. He'd felt anger and sympathy stir. Dangerous undercurrents when this woman was his rival for Ariane.

She was challenging, dangerous. Around her his emotions became stronger, more unwieldy.

Through her story he'd felt horror, sympathy and outrage but even now he didn't know whether she'd manipulated him. Her story was far-fetched and he wanted to dismiss it as fantasy. Except no one was that good an actor. He'd not only seen but felt her distress and pain.

There was a chance her story was true.

When she'd talked of her lying scum boyfriend her expression had revealed bitter betrayal and Jake had felt the urge to smash the guy's face. His skin crawled at the idea of her father keeping her captive, cut off from friends.

As for stealing her baby... Surely no father would do that!

Yet Jake knew that simply having children didn't make someone a caring parent. His mother was a case in point.

Had Caro given him a sob story to win him over

while she found a way to get Ariane? Watching that challenging stare, he was torn between doubt and the desire to believe.

And desire of a different kind, for carnal pleasure. Their quick coupling hadn't eradicated it. Instead it was as if one taste of her no-holds-barred passion left him addicted.

It was appallingly difficult to focus on the past.

Had she abandoned Ariane or had her daughter been stolen? That was the crux of the matter. If she was lying she was the best liar he'd ever met. His gut told him she spoke the truth. Yet he needed evidence.

'I'll reserve judgement till I have proof you didn't give her away.'

Instead of her being downcast at his words, her expression lightened. 'I'll arrange a meeting with the midwife.'

She looked almost excited. The contrast with her earlier vulnerability was almost painful to observe. Surely that meant he could trust her.

Except people could be bought, stories altered.

'You do that.'

Jake wouldn't easily be convinced. He clenched his jaw against the wild see-saw of emotions. He was used to assessing situations quickly, trusting his instinct and taking decisive action. This uncertainty, the conflict between his desire to believe and the knowledge he couldn't, yet, was maddening.

'Well...' for the first time since she'd stormed out of the gala she looked uncertain '... I suppose it's time you returned to the ball. Do you need me to show you the way?'

Jake frowned. 'I'm not interested in the ball. I only came here to see you.'

The words echoed with a profound resonance. It was truer than he'd thought. Even now, when he knew he'd get no further proof tonight, he was magnetised by her. He didn't want to leave.

Whether it was the sexily mussed look of her ripe lips, untidy hair and crumpled dress, or the deeper thread of sympathy stirred by her story, Jake didn't know. But he felt…connected, drawn to her. Though he couldn't allow himself to trust her.

His voice must have revealed his doubt. He saw her react, her pupils dilate and her body sway infinitesimally nearer, till she jerked back.

'It's late. There's no proof I can give you tonight.'

'You want me to go?'

Caro felt her eyes widen as Jake's low voice rumbled through her.

She opened her mouth to say of course she wanted him to leave. He'd been brutally insulting. He'd made her feel like dirt.

Right before he'd made her feel as if she'd found heaven.

A squiggle of arousal stirred deep inside and she rubbed her damp palms down her skirt. Jake's eyes tracked the movement. To her dismay her nipples budded against her silk bodice while between her legs that slow circling ache of want started up anew.

Caro swallowed. She tried to summon a convenient lie. *Yes, I want you to go.* But her tongue didn't co-operate.

'Caro?' That gravel-wrapped-in-velvet voice reminded her of the night she'd kissed him and he'd held her while she cried. It was rough yet tender and strangely reassuring. It shouldn't be. They were on opposing sides.

'I—'

'Because I don't want to leave.' His features took on a grim cast, the planes of his face stark and sheer.

'What *do* you want?' The words came this time, breathless and quick.

'You.' He didn't move closer but it felt as if he did. As if he'd reached out and trailed his hand over her flesh, awakening dangerous longing. 'Us. Together. Again.'

'You despise me.' She summoned her pride as a last defence against his appalling power to tempt her. He'd flayed her with his insults. She wouldn't forget that soon.

He shook his head. 'I did, before you told me what happened.'

'You're saying you believe me?' It couldn't be so easy.

She was right. 'I told you, I'll reserve judgement till I have proof.'

He drew a slow breath and for the first time she realised he was as tense as she. His big chest rose in a shudder and the muscles in his jaw worked as if he held himself back with difficulty. 'But I still want you. More than ever.'

The words, delivered not in challenge but with devastating honesty, loosened her knees. Caro snatched in air to her overworked lungs but couldn't fill them.

'I've wanted you from the moment you sashayed into my office looking ridiculously sexy in that brown

outfit. You made me feel like some Victorian repro-
bate, lusting after the staff.'

Caro stepped back in shock, straight into the window embrasure.

'You were attracted then?'

The voice of self-preservation told her it didn't matter. Nothing mattered but Ariane. Yet it wasn't true.
This—whatever it was between her and Jake—was so
powerful she felt it at a visceral level. In his arms Caro
felt renewed, happy, vibrantly alive.

It made her weak when she needed to be strong. But
oh, what weakness!

Even angry, desperate sex with this man had felt
profound.

Surely it was a catastrophic mistake to give in to it,
yet it felt anything but wrong.

'You couldn't tell?' He stepped close and she felt
hot all over from that silvery stare. 'I thought it was
obvious.' Another deep breath. This time that broad
chest came within a hair's breadth of her breasts and
she had to fight not to lean into him.

Caro shook her head. 'Sex would complicate things
between us.'

Jake's mouth rucked up at one side in a disarming smile that turned her insides molten. 'A bit late to
worry about, don't you think?' He paused. 'Whatever
the rights and wrongs, we find ourselves in a…fraught
situation. Why not indulge in a little recreational pleasure to relieve the tension?'

He made it sound not only logical but laudable. This
man was incredibly dangerous!

And yet… She wanted badly to put aside her hurt,
even for a short time.

'And afterwards? We part as enemies?'

He lifted his hand, feathering one finger down her cheek, then across to her mouth where her lips promptly opened for him. Heat drilled deep inside and she shuddered as she inhaled the citrus and male scent of his skin.

'How about we call a truce?' he purred. 'Till the negotiations begin.'

It was absurd. Reckless and irresponsible.

Utterly tempting.

Caro shuddered, her senses on overdrive. She told herself to be sensible. She opened her mouth to spurn him and heard herself say, 'Perhaps just once.'

The words were barely out when he scooped her into his arms. He carried her as easily as if he did it every day, leaving her hyper-aware of his strength and a sense of well-being. It was crazy but nevertheless real.

Then they were in the bedroom and he put her on her feet, reaching to flick on a bedside lamp. Caro waited for the frenzy of need, the urgent hands, hard on her body, that had so excited her before.

Instead, to her surprise, Jake lifted his hands to her hair. Gently, with deft patience, he drew out the pins that secured her tiara and kept her hair up. He wore a lazy half-smile as his fingers moved in her hair in a series of caresses that made her shiver all over.

Finally he removed the delicate tiara but instead of stopping, those hard hands massaged her scalp, turning her boneless. The exquisite sensations, the unhurried intent in those glittering eyes and the stroke of his breath on her skin turned it into the most amazing foreplay.

Caro's head fell back, her hair cascading in waves

around her shoulders. She clutched his upper arms as he kissed her jaw, her throat and down, down, down to the low-sitting line of her bodice.

That was only the beginning. Caro had expected fast and hard. What she got was endless patience and a sure sensuality that made her realise how limited her experience was. Mike had never seduced her with such infinite patience, or with such devastating knowledge of how to excite her.

By the time they were on the bed, he in boxers and she in nothing at all, she was quivering with anticipation, her breath coming in broken snatches. Finally, unable to wait, she reached for him, hand closing around his fabric-covered erection.

'Wait.' Hard fingers encircled hers and she saw Jake grimace as he throbbed against her touch. 'We need a condom.' His ragged voice made her realise that in this passion they were equals.

She almost smiled till his words sank in.

'I don't have any.'

He frowned, head turning to the bedside table.

'Not there. Not anywhere.' She pulled her hand away, feeling almost embarrassed. As if it were a crime to be celibate! 'I don't have sex.'

Jake stared as if he'd never seen her before. Because he hadn't believed her when she'd said there'd been no one but Mike? But before she had time to take offence, his mouth curled up in a sexy grin that made her heart leap against her ribs and her throat jam.

'You do now, Princess.' He kissed her quickly but with a naked intent that had her writhing beneath him.

Then suddenly she was bereft as he rose and reached

for his trousers. Moments later he was naked, rolling a condom onto his impressive erection.

Caro swallowed hard, overwhelmed by her need for this magnificent man. She told herself her emotions were more profound because of the intense circumstances, the roller coaster of hope and fear since she'd heard Ariane was alive. But as Jake met her eyes and that ponderous pulse of connection pounded between them, Caro feared it was more.

He came to her, held her, kissed her, then, despite his arousal, slowly explored her with his mouth and hands. By the time he reached her sex, his breath a caress, she couldn't take any more.

'No!' He lifted his head and Caro stared, overwhelmed, at the sight of him there between her legs. One more touch and… 'I want *you*.'

'I haven't finished—'

Raising herself on her elbow, she reached for him, her hand sliding through the dark silk of his hair. 'Please.'

The teasing light in his eyes faded, replaced by something that felt heavy in her chest. Something warm and almost reassuring. Jake prowled up her body and carnal excitement stifled everything else.

This time when they came together it was slow and sure and almost familiar as he held her gaze and she held him. This time the fizz of sparks didn't explode as fast but the way their bodies rocked together, the searing strands of fire threading through her at every movement, every breath, every touch, made the climax more compelling.

Caro's orgasm bore down upon her, first in tiny ripples that made Jake's eyes glint with approval. Then in great undulating waves that made her cling and bite her lip against the urge to cry out.

She hung suspended, held from oblivion only by that grey gaze. Then his wide shoulders quaked, he flung his head back and powered deep inside and ecstasy took her.

CHAPTER TWELVE

JAKE WOKE ALONE in her bed.

Daylight streamed in yet he couldn't bring himself to move. Caro's 'perhaps just once' had turned into a long, vigorous night. Good thing he'd had condoms in his wallet. The more he had her, the more he wanted, and Caro had been equally needy.

Now he was content to wait for her to emerge from the bathroom.

Last night's madness could have been a major error. The last thing he needed, if it did come to a court case, was a sexual relationship with Princess Carolina muddying the waters.

Yet he couldn't regret that amazing night.

His belly warmed at the memory of her coming apart in his arms, her generous passion and his exultation. Caro had been everything he desired, though more than once he'd observed surprise at some of his caresses, and his ability to bring her multiple climaxes. Ego suggested the quality of his lovemaking surprised her but he suspected she really had been pretty inexperienced.

Which put an intriguing slant on what she'd told him. Some of it was true, possibly most of it. But he couldn't accept it all without proof, despite what felt like the best sex of his life.

It was tempting to believe they'd shared something extraordinary. His sated body and the smile tugging his lips confirmed it. But Jake was cautious. He preferred to ascribe this feeling to a particularly compatible woman and recent celibacy.

Jake surveyed his surroundings, curious at the difference between this room and the rest of the palace. Despite its high ceilings, ornate plasterwork and spacious dimensions, it wasn't as opulent. The furnishings looked comfortable, the fabric on the armchair in a shaft of sunlight actually looked frayed.

Probably because Caro only stayed here occasionally. But the bookcase on one wall, stuffed full, proved it was more than a convenient bolthole. Intrigued, he investigated.

Children's books jostled with classics and tomes on art. On one shelf was a stack of sketch books. He plucked one, leafing through and discovering drawings of formal gardens, a servant in livery and a bird on a branch.

He turned, looking for information about the woman he'd spent the night with. Nearby was a single framed photo. The resemblance was so intense Jake's pulse jumped.

Picking it up, he saw a woman of about thirty with Caro's slim build. Her hair was red but not Caro's dark auburn. This woman's was lighter, matching Ariane's, and her eyes, deep violet with that familiar slanting angle that made them look mysterious and happy at the same time, looked like Ariane's eyes, and Caro's.

This must be Caro's mother. Ariane's grandmother.

She held a baby with a fuzz of reddish hair, one tiny hand reaching towards her mother.

Abruptly Jake put the photo down, recalling Neil's report on Princess Carolina. She'd lost her mother when she was tiny. Her father remarried almost immediately. This photo seemed to indicate a bond with a mother she could barely have known, rather than with the woman who'd raised her.

He thought about Ariane losing her adoptive parents. And Caro's story of having Ariane stolen from her.

What if it were true?

What if the passionate woman he'd bedded wasn't a spoiled princess who hadn't wanted her child? What if she'd genuinely believed her child dead, the maternal bond broken, as with her own mother?

Something lodged in Jake's belly. A weight that, against the laws of physics, rose within him, crushing his lungs and stopping his breath.

He swung around, needing to find her. She'd been in the bathroom a long time. Too long.

Jake walked past a wooden-faced footman on the ground floor. Either the servants were used to guests ending the night in a royal bed, or too well trained to bat an eye. He didn't care. What he cared about was locating Caro.

His need to find her had grown from a niggle to a presentiment of trouble. No matter how unaccustomed she was to nights of passion, it was unlike the woman he knew not to face him this morning. His nape tightened.

Finally, when he was almost at the ballroom, he

heard a loud voice. Pushing open a not quite closed door, he found himself in an empty sitting room. On the far side French windows stood open to the garden. Following the sound of voices, Jake stepped outside then realised the conversation was taking place in the next room. He moved to another set of French windows and looked inside. It was a study with gilded antiques and floor-to-ceiling books that looked, unlike the ones in Caro's room, as if they'd never been opened. The occupants didn't notice him on the threshold.

King Hugo of St Ancilla sat behind an oversized desk. Caro stood before him in a tailored skirt and jacket, spine straight and chin up. Jake silently applauded her, for the monarch wasn't holding back his tirade in mixed English and Ancillan. Jake's stomach curdled at his blistering vitriol.

He was about to make himself known when Caro spoke.

'I did what you insisted, came back and attended every event this week. As for leaving early last night…' She shrugged. 'I'm not here to discuss that.'

'How *dare* you speak to me like that?' The King's face darkened.

'Oh, I *dare*, Father.' Amazingly Caro's defiant tone made the King stop, eyes widening. 'I only came here because you threatened to send your goons to haul me back, and, in the process, wreck my plans.'

'Plans? You don't have plans. You spend your time playing at being a preschool teacher. It's time you toed the line and came home.' He sat back, an ugly smile on his face. 'I've a mind to organise your wedding next. There's a banker in the US I'm cultivating.' His tone turned sneering. 'I know your weakness for Americans.'

Any thought Jake had of revealing his presence died as Caro turned parchment-pale. She wouldn't thank him for witnessing this.

Besides, it could be his chance to discover whether she'd told him the truth.

'Or perhaps the Australian you spent the night with. We could turn your scandalous behaviour to advantage, put pressure on him to come up to scratch. His fortune is huge.'

Jake was absorbing that when Caro stepped up to the desk. She slapped her hands down and leaned forward.

'Make your plans for my brothers, not me. I wash my hands of you.' She drew a deep breath and Jake, seeing the light glinting on her bright hair, realised she was shaking. 'I know what you did. The lies you told, the laws you broke.'

For a moment the King said nothing. When he spoke his voice was venomous. 'Careful, Carolina. I've let you go your own way for years but I can bring you to heel like that.' He snapped his fingers.

Slowly she shook her head. 'Not this time. Not any more.' She straightened, her hands clenched. 'You stole my child. You had her illegally adopted without my consent.'

Jake's hand closed so hard on the door frame that pain shot from his palm up his arm.

It was true. Unbelievably it was true.

His mind boggled and his stomach dropped.

He'd got her so wrong.

The things he'd said last night!

Jake rocked back as guilt and horror filled him.

'There was never any question of you keeping it.'

'Her. I had a girl.'

'A bastard.' Her father shrugged. 'As if I'd allow that blot on the family name. I did what I did for the family. You should be grateful—'

'Grateful? Hardly. I know where she is and I'm going to get her. We're going to live together. I'm going to raise my daughter the way a child *should* be raised and—'

'You'll do no such thing. Put the idea from your head right now. Unless you'd like another year living under guard till you see sense?'

Jake couldn't take any more. He rapped on the window frame, feigning a smile as they whipped round towards him.

'Good morning, Your Majesty… Carolina. I hope I'm not interrupting.' He paused, looking from one to the other, willing Caro to follow his lead. She looked pale, her features drawn.

He'd heard enough to suspect that, with only a little more provocation, her father would have her clapped in a dungeon or a tower, guarded by sentries. Jake recalled her bleak expression when she'd spoken of being held against her will by the King's security men. Until he could get her out of St Ancilla, she wouldn't be safe.

Jake didn't question his determination to get her away. She'd told the truth. He owed her more than an apology for last night's scathing words.

'Not at all.' The King recovered first, stretching his mouth into a smile like a hungry shark's.

'I'm so glad.' Jake stepped into the room, standing beside Caro and planting his palm reassuringly at her back. She shivered and he had to bite back the words he longed to fling at her father. Instead he made himself smile. 'Carolina promised to show me something of the countryside today, didn't you, darling?'

She blinked, her brow furrowing at his words. Before she could speak Jake ploughed on.

'I must thank you, Your Highness, for the invitation to last night's event. It was spectacular. I'm honoured to have been invited.' He smiled as if his one aim in life were to hang out with pampered aristocrats, then added the bait. 'Especially as I understand there are some interesting investment opportunities in your country.'

Ignoring Caro's scowl, he watched the King and saw his ruse had worked. Perhaps Neil was right and the royal coffers weren't as plump as they used to be. He'd noticed a number of high-profile financiers attending last night, including a few involved in his latest project. It wouldn't hurt if the King thought he planned to stay and look at business options.

'It was our pleasure to have you here.' No sign of a scowl now on that crimson face. 'You must accept our hospitality for the rest of your visit.'

'You're most kind, Your Highness.' Jake slipped his hand from Caro's back to capture her hand. He squeezed it reassuringly. 'I'd hoped to make an early start on our sightseeing. Unless...'

He let his words trail off as he gave Caro a melting smile. Best if her father thought he was unaware of the dark undercurrents in the room.

'Of course. Carolina, see you take Mr Maynard to the business park on the way out of the city.'

Caro opened her mouth and Jake spoke first. 'That sounds perfect. But maybe on the way back. There are other sights Carolina promised to show me first.'

'I'm sure there are.' The King's suggestive chuckle curdled Jake's belly but he kept his expression light.

Finally, to his relief, Caro spoke up. 'That's right. We'd better leave now if we're to fit everything in.'

'Come and see me when you return, Carolina.' It wasn't a suggestion but an order.

Jake wore a calm face as they traversed the palace. He was determined the servants wouldn't see anything amiss, though restraining his seething emotions took concentration. Caro's hand was cold in his and she moved stiffly, shoulders high and face blank.

He was torn between slashing guilt over the way he'd treated her, disbelief at the enormity of what he'd witnessed and the desire to do serious damage to the man they'd just left.

Jake had thought his own mother appalling. She had nothing on Caro's father.

They remained silent till they reached Caro's rooms. As the door shut, Jake wrapped his arms around her, breath expelling in a rush when she didn't push him away. He didn't deserve her trust.

His scorn last night proved he had no filter and precious little control where Caro was concerned. He'd told himself he was furious on Ariane's behalf but this was more, much more.

Caro leaned close, fracturing his thoughts and filling him with relief. He inhaled spice and woman, her hair tickling his cheek, her body warm and trembling.

His arms tightened. 'I'm getting you out of here. Now.'

Caro let Jake lead her from the helipad along the path to the castle. She'd been away less than a week yet spring had arrived in the Alps. The air was warm and the snow had begun melting. Further down the slope she saw the first traces of wildflowers. The air felt fresh with promise and the fragrance of growing things teased her nostrils.

While she felt chilled.

Everything had happened quickly. Maybe she was in shock. The confrontation with her father, then Jake spiriting her off St Ancilla in a private jet, followed by this short hop in a helicopter. She wasn't used to anyone, especially a man, coming to her rescue. That added to the air of unreality.

If ever she'd doubted Jake's ability to make things happen, today would have disabused her. He'd made one call while she gathered her most precious possessions in a large shoulder bag. Her mother's photo, her mother's jewellery that she'd worn last night and some illustrated books she'd had when she was young and had always wanted to give her own child. Then they were heading to the garages and from there to an airfield.

All the time fear tingled down her spine as she imagined her father's reaction when he found her gone.

She had no illusions that his threat to hold her by force was bluster. He was ruthless. While she was in St Ancilla he had all the power, despite what the law said.

'I have to thank you. Getting me off the island.' She stopped and turned to Jake as the helicopter lifted off and its throbbing thunder retreated.

He looked the same, dark-featured, broad-shouldered and with the air of calm competence that reassured.

Alarms tripped in her brain, warning that she

couldn't relax her guard, couldn't rely on anyone but herself. Yet it was too late. She'd gone so far with him, in so many ways, she couldn't pretend none of it had happened.

It felt as if a lifetime had passed since they met.

'There's no need for thanks. I was glad to get away too.'

There was so much to discuss but neither was eager to start. They'd barely spoken on the trip. Caro because she grappled with a barrage of emotions and Jake because he was busy working on his phone. Because his business couldn't wait or because he realised she needed some quiet time?

Pewter-grey eyes surveyed her. 'You're feeling better now you're off St Ancilla?'

Caro breathed deep and nodded, looking away to the magnificent vista of fields, forests and soaring mountains. On the other side of the valley towering waterfalls, fed by melting snow, plunged to the valley floor.

'I wouldn't have got away so easily without your help.' She faced the horrible truth today had revealed. 'I love my country but I can't stay there. Not with my father's threats hanging over me. If he sends his men after me...'

She shivered and hunched her shoulders despite the warm sunlight on her back. To be virtually exiled from her homeland was bad enough. To fear returning because it could only be on the King's terms was even worse.

'Don't worry. I've got people working on it.' Caro raised her eyebrows but before she could question Jake continued. 'Let's talk about it later. For now just know you're safe.' He gestured to the castle, golden in the sunlight, its machicolated towers charming yet sturdy, its massive walls solid. 'I'll make sure no one, not even the King of St Ancilla, can harm you or Ariane here.'

'Thank you. That's…good of you.'

It meant everything to have breathing space to decide what to do next. To know her daughter, and she, were safe for now.

Caro felt stiff facial muscles twinge as she smiled. 'You're sure you're the same man who stalked into the palace last night with vengeance in his eyes?'

He'd looked like an avenging angel.

There was no answering humour in Jake's features. If anything he looked even grimmer.

Warmth enveloped her hand and she looked down to see he'd captured it in both of his. Heat radiated from his touch and the tension stringing her muscles began to ease.

'I owe you an apology.' Jake winced. 'I jumped to conclusions about you that were unfounded and hurtful. Can you forgive me? I cringe when I think of what I said. The way I treated you, in private and in front of others. You didn't deserve that. I lost control and I'm ashamed.'

Caro read his remorse. His words, his contempt, had hurt. Badly. With a lancing pain that drove right to her heart. But he hadn't known the truth.

'I can't blame you for doubting my word. I came here in disguise, lying to you.' She paused. 'I apologise for that. My only excuse is I was desperate, scared I'd lose the chance to see my daughter.' Caro tried to summon a smile but it felt like a grimace. 'I was afraid if I told you who I was you'd stop me seeing her when I'd just learned she was alive.'

'Caro, you don't—'

'I do have to explain. I hated lying. I knew soon enough that you loved her and wanted to protect her, but I knew you'd see me as an enemy, particularly when I told my story. It was so far-fetched. You were right, it does sound like something from an old story.' The sort that had evil stepmothers and awful curses.

Caro's stepmother wasn't evil. Just wrapped up in her own family with no warmth to share for another woman's child. As for her father, he was larger than life with his selfish, manipulative ways and towering temper.

Not for the first time she wondered what life would have been like if her mother had lived. Everyone said she was gentle yet fun-loving. Caro had a horrible feeling life with her royal husband would have been hellish.

'Nevertheless, I should have waited to be sure of the facts.' Jake's stern voice sliced her thoughts. 'Abandoning children is a hot button for me. I saw red and acted before thinking. Believe it or not, that's not my usual way.'

He looked down to where his thumb described a half circle again and again on the back of her hand. He seemed so abstracted she guessed he had no idea of the powerful, delicious sensations his caress evoked.

Here she was, fleeing her country, her father and her King, with her life in chaos. Yet she found it impossible to concentrate on her problems because of Jake Maynard and the feelings he evoked.

She tugged her hand free, ignoring that twitch of dark eyebrows.

She cradled her fingers, warm from his touch, in her other hand. 'Don't worry. I'm tougher than I look.'

She'd had to be. 'I'm not about to collapse in tears or have a breakdown.'

Caro was acutely aware of the fact Jake had seen her at her lowest ebb, unable to stop the grief she'd carried for so long. She'd wept in his arms, finding a solace she'd never known before. But she wouldn't do that again. The humiliation of having him witness that scene with her father still cramped her insides. Even though it had convinced Jake she told the truth, she hated him thinking she was a helpless victim.

His smile when it came was crooked but totally disarming. It set light to her last defences like flame to paper. She could almost hear the whoosh of conflagration as her resistance crumbled to ashes.

'It seems those stories about your breakdown years ago were exaggerated.' His smile died and Caro read concern in his smoky gaze. 'You don't have to convince me you're strong, Caro. To get through what you did, to keep going, and deal with *him*…' He shook his head. 'That takes guts.'

Caro's heart swelled. It was the first time she'd received such a compliment. 'I've never held my own against him before. I let him—'

'Don't!' Jake raised a palm to stop her. 'Don't blame yourself. He was your father and your King and he held all the power.'

Jake's stare pinioned hers. Instead of her feeling cornered, her confidence rose, a warm glow that felt like happiness.

They stood, gazes locked. Caro didn't want to move. The quality of Jake's regard, how he made her feel about herself, were new and precious.

'I've got one question.' His voice made her blink.

'Yes?' Absurdly, now the worst was over, she was breathless.

'Do I have to call you Carolina now?'

She smiled and took a half step back, suddenly aware she'd canted towards him. 'I've come to loathe my full name. My father insists on it but as he's usually in a bad mood he makes it sound ugly. My friends call me Caro.'

Jake bent forward in a formal bow as if he were a master of court etiquette. 'May I call you Caro?'

Did that mean he saw her as his friend?

Caro wasn't sure whether to be pleased. She should be. It meant he trusted her. Yet given her deep-seated, confusing feelings for him, 'friend' was such a lukewarm word.

'Of course.' Looking into his eyes, she felt a zap of energy that warned she was vulnerable to this man. Hurriedly she gathered her wits. 'And now? What happens next?'

Caro would call her friends in St Ancilla and her lawyer, to warn them the King would be on a rampage when he discovered she'd left. She didn't think he'd take out his wrath on them but he could be unstable when crossed.

'Next?' Jake's smile was easy. 'We'll work it out one step at a time. There's no rush. For now concentrate on the fact you and Ariane are safe.'

Caro swallowed. He didn't want her thanks yet he gave her so much, refuge when she needed it most. They still had to work out Ariane's future. Ostensibly they were on opposing sides, yet Jake treated her as someone to be protected.

The knowledge stirred the most poignant feelings. Here was a man she could respect as well as…

'And us? Is there an us?' Instinctively she lifted her chin, ready to pretend it didn't matter if he said last night's passion had been a mistake.

Jake's face turned unreadable.

She'd give anything to know what he thought. Did he regret having sex? Was it gauche and embarrassing to mention it now they'd moved on from those moments of heightened emotion?

She wished she knew one-night-stand etiquette.

'Do you want there to be?'

Caro had imagined this morning that confronting her hectoring father would take all her courage. Yet, looking into that piercing gaze that gave nothing away, her heart thudding against her ribs, she discovered her courage could still be tested.

She craved more of what she'd experienced with Jake, that soul-searing passion that went beyond anything she'd known. Yet with everything so uncertain—

'It's okay. You don't need to answer now, Caro. Shall we take that one step at a time too?'

She slicked her dry lips, searching for the right words when a shout made her turn.

Rounding the corner of the castle were Jake's secretary Neil and Ariane, hopping beside him.

Abruptly it hit her, the fact that she was here, safe for now from her father's machinations and with her daughter. Her incredible, lovely daughter. Caro's breath shuddered through her as relief and joy filled her.

'Come on, Caro.' She felt Jake's hand warm at the small of her back. 'It's time to see your little girl.'

CHAPTER THIRTEEN

Jake surveyed the pair sitting across from him and fought to hide his response to the picture they made.

Ariane had begun the trip down the mountain's steep cog railway on the seat beside Caro. But as Caro pointed through the carriage window, his niece had climbed onto her lap. Now Caro's arm rested around Ariane's middle as they chattered about the view and the quaint Alpine farmhouses.

His ribs tightened at their glow of happiness. His niece and her mother. Not that Ariane knew Caro was her mother. They'd agreed to keep that quiet till Ariane was better able to understand.

But she was still his niece and always would be.

His lawyers said there were legal arguments on both sides, for him as Ariane's permanent guardian, and for Caro as birth mother. Though they thought, despite the wrong done years ago, they could successfully argue that the continuity of living with him would be best for Ariane.

Jake felt no triumph at the news.

He didn't *want* a legal wrangle with Caro.

He watched their faces, alight with pleasure as Caro spotted hikers with a frolicking dog. Two shades of red hair, one coppery and the other a deep, ruby auburn, touched as they craned to look. Two sets of violet eyes and two smiles, each capable of twisting his heart.

He wanted Ariane with him. And he wanted Caro.

The twist of heat moved from his chest to his groin. He *had* Caro. She'd been his lover ever since St Ancilla.

That first night back he'd been surprised by the rap on his door. When he'd found Caro there, huddled in a robe with her hair in waves around her shoulders, he'd pulled her inside, expecting to hear her appalling father had managed, despite Jake's precautions, to contact her with threats.

It had taken all Jake's once considerable restraint to hold back from her, invite her to sit, turn his brain to tactics to stymie the King's machinations.

But instead of talking about her father or Ariane, Caro had surprised him. Gone was the wan woman who'd left St Ancilla beside him. Instead he'd been visited by the ardent siren who'd given herself so generously the night before.

Had he held back? Worried about taking advantage when he knew she'd been rocked by recent experiences?

Jake counted himself a decent guy, if hard-nosed in business. But he wasn't into self-abnegation. He'd hauled Caro into his bed. For the last ten days he'd made sure she was satisfied, more than satisfied, there.

He truly was selfish. He had Caro each night and still he wanted more. He had no name for this craving. To possess her physically. But more too. To bask in her smiles. Enjoy her in ways that had little to do with sex.

'Uncle Jake…?'

He found two pairs of eyes on him.

'Sorry?' He yanked his thoughts to the present. Their trip up the mountain. His sense of victory when he'd finally persuaded Caro it was safe to take Ariane out. That her father's henchmen couldn't grab them. Even then she hadn't relaxed till his own security staff boarded the next carriage, keeping a discreet distance.

Jake hated the need for such a precaution but the deeper the experts dug, the less he trusted the King to behave reasonably. He'd do whatever it took to keep Ariane and Caro from the monarch's reach.

'What are you thinking, Uncle Jake? You look funny.'

'Do I?' He met Ariane's bright eyes, so like her mother's, and felt his fluency desert him. His brain went completely blank. Because he'd been thinking about sex with Caro and how his need for her kept growing, not diminishing with familiarity.

'This sort of funny?' he asked as he crossed his eyes.

Ariane giggled and the tight sensation in his chest eased. He loved hearing her happy.

'Or this?' He stuck his tongue in his cheek and scrunched his eyebrows down.

His gaze caught Caro's. She was smiling, the shadows he sometimes saw in her eyes banished.

Elation hit. By rights it should be because he was finally on the verge of closing the deal he'd come to Switzerland to accomplish. Or because he might have found a way to protect Caro and Ariane from the King long term. Instead this burst of happiness came from the sight of Caro's eyes, dancing with approval as he made a fool of himself in front of a bunch of tourists.

The realisation shook him. Her smile and her approval had such power.

What did that mean?

And what did he intend to do about it?

Caro lay on her back, heart pounding, legs weak as overcooked pasta and a smile of well-being curving her lips. How often had she felt like this in Jake's bed, basking in the afterglow of his loving?

The man had a knack for diverting her worries about the future and her conniving father. And the sight of Ariane growing more confident and loving proved that good things *could* happen.

They hadn't discussed Ariane's future. It had been enough to know she was safe from the King. Despite furious messages from her father Jake had somehow managed to convince him to keep his distance. But they'd have to face their problems. Caro wasn't naïve enough to believe this state of glorious limbo could continue.

Zoe had rung today, warning again that winning custody of Ariane wouldn't be simple. She favoured a negotiated arrangement with Jake. Which suited Caro. She couldn't imagine them on opposing sides in court. Yet nor could she envisage Ariane living part time with her and part with Jake, possibly on the other side of the world.

She should be relieved Jake hadn't forced the issue. Yet they couldn't go on like this despite his insistence that for now Ariane needed calm and stability. But Caro had never found the right time to shatter this peaceful interlude.

Caro rolled onto her side and watched the early light

gild the mountains. She'd found peace here, such happiness, she didn't want it to end. Not only for Ariane but for *her*.

The bathroom door opened and there Jake was, naked but for a towel around his hips, his hair damp and the muscles in that glorious torso shifting as he moved. Despite her satiation Caro felt the tug of attraction deep inside.

Longing for him filled her yet she knew their peaceful bubble must shatter. Was today the day?

'You're awake?' He approached, smiling, and she smiled back, almost accustomed to the fillip of joy gathering behind her breastbone. No one, ever, had made her feel the way Jake did. The thought lodged and Caro stilled as its implications penetrated.

'Something wrong?' He watched her as she struggled to stifle a sudden, disquieting idea.

'No, nothing.' She made a production of turning to plump up pillows behind her and sit up, drawing the sheet under her arms. By the time she faced him again she had her calm face on, the one she'd learned in the palace, forged under the lash of her father's contempt and her stepmother's disapproval.

Yet her heart pounded wildly and perspiration prickled her hairline. Her powers of concealment weren't as good as she'd hoped for Jake sat beside her, frowning. He took her hand and she experienced that familiar jolt of delight.

'Are you worried about a possible pregnancy? Because of that first night?'

Heat blossomed in her cheeks. 'It's unlikely, given the timing.' That was what she'd told herself again and again. 'Time enough to worry about that if it happens.'

'You wouldn't be alone, Caro.' His thumb stroked the back of her hand. 'I'd look after you. I don't abandon my responsibilities.'

And that, Caro realised as her heart landed somewhere near the floor, was part of the problem. She didn't want to be a responsibility to Jake. Nor did she want to be a rival for Ariane. She wanted to be someone he—

'I was going to wait till later but now's as good a time as any. We need to talk, Caro.'

His gentle tone, the way he watched her, assessing her reaction, made her heart skip. Tension crawled along her shoulders to the back of her neck. Was he going to say he'd decided he couldn't give Ariane up?

It was stupid to jump to conclusions but a lifetime of disappointment, of things going against her, had conditioned Caro to expect the worst. She tugged her hand free and folded her arms over her chest.

'I agree. We can't continue this way indefinitely.'

Keen eyes surveyed her. What did he see? She had the unnerving notion he saw far more than she'd like.

'My time in Switzerland is almost over. The project I've been working on is complete.'

Caro's eyes widened. Despite telling herself this wasn't permanent, she hadn't thought about Jake leaving. Distress coated her tongue.

'It's not long term?'

He had investments globally. From the snippets she'd heard between him and Neil she'd imagined his current work continuing.

He shrugged. 'It is, but now everything's in place I don't need to be here. My role was to cajole the other investors into participating.'

Caro frowned. 'Is that normal? Moving from place to place with each new investment?'

Jake shrugged. 'This wasn't business in the usual sense. It's a pet project. I had to chivvy reluctant investors.'

'Surely if you can prove they'll make a good return they'd agree.'

'You're assuming the investors would reap the financial rewards.'

Now Caro really was intrigued, despite the low-grade frisson of nerves, reminding her they had more personal things to discuss. Was that why she was eager to talk business? To put off the evil moment?

'You make it sound like a great mystery.'

He laughed. 'No, at least not now we've got agreement. I developed a self-perpetuating investment scheme. But instead of profits returning to investors they'll be channelled into programmes for child victims of war and natural disaster. I came here to lobby some powerful corporations and governments. Especially corporations that need to rehabilitate their reputations as global citizens.'

'Companies that could do with positive press?' Caro could name a few. 'You tapped into the high-level talks here to establish a charity?'

The region regularly hosted talks between governments and attracted lobbyists from some of the world's most powerful corporations.

'There's nothing like face to face meetings to drive a project, especially when you're asking for substantial sums they'll never see again.'

Caro sat back, taking in the satisfaction on Jake's

face. He glowed like a man who'd sealed a deal to make his fortune. Instead the deal was for others.

'Why children? Why in war zones?'

'Not just war. In areas hit by tsunamis, hurricanes, any large-scale disorder.' His eyes held hers. 'You don't think it a good cause?'

'I think it's wonderful. I'm just curious.'

She'd thought she knew Jake. Living with him and Ariane, seeing him with his staff, she'd discovered many sides to his character. This was something new. He loved Ariane but she'd thought that was because he was her uncle. Maybe there was more to his motivation.

His gaze slid to the window. 'I spent a few years in the army. We were deployed in the Asia Pacific region mopping up after natural disasters, and once after a civil war. Some of the children…'

He stopped and Caro realised he wasn't seeing the glorious Swiss scenery. Her heart squeezed as his features tightened.

'Children are the most vulnerable, especially if separated from family. It can take years to reunite kids with remaining family, if there *is* any. Most disaster support is for food and shelter. Only a few agencies address the longer term process of finding secure, loving homes for lost children.'

Caro heard emotion beneath his words. She recalled images of disaster-ravaged zones worldwide and shuddered, imagining Ariane alone and lost.

Jake must have seen her shiver. His hand covered hers. This time she didn't object.

'What you're doing is important. Clever too, to target the big companies to contribute.'

'It will be good PR for them.'

Caro guessed Jake wouldn't claim any of those kudos. She wanted to say she was proud of him but stopped herself. She had no right to sound proprietorial, even if she felt it.

After her earlier revelation she needed to be careful.

'I didn't know you'd been in the army,' she said, trying to distract herself.

'It wasn't a long career. I didn't have the temperament for being ordered about.' At her questioning look he said, 'I got into trouble as a kid and my sister convinced me it was a ticket out of the place we lived.'

No mistaking his bitterness. 'You weren't happy at home?'

Reading the tension in those broad shoulders, she wondered if he'd answer. But eventually his lips curved in a rueful smile. 'It probably wasn't too bad but I was trouble. A misfit. My sister told me if I didn't sort myself out I'd end up in gaol. I was starting to act out.'

'Your sister, not your parents?'

Gunmetal-grey eyes met hers. 'I never knew my father and my mother abandoned us on a regular basis. She only came home when her latest boyfriend dumped her. The last time she left I was barely fourteen but Connie looked after me, stopped me from going into foster care.'

The air whooshed from Caro's lungs. No wonder he had a thing about lost children. And women abandoning their kids. She remembered his lacerating words when he thought she'd abandoned Ariane. No wonder he'd been so savage.

'Yes.' He nodded, as if reading her thoughts. 'I've got baggage. Usually I keep it under wraps. But with you...' He shook his head. 'It was like a red rag to a bull. I'm sorry I—'

'Don't.' Caro put her hand up. 'It's in the past. So you went into the army. That's a far cry from finance.'

Jake spread his hands. 'The army taught me discipline and that there was a big world out there. It gave me the drive to work hard and improve. Then my sister and I had a windfall. There were plans for a giant shopping complex in our suburb but the planners forgot to acquire a small parcel of land.' He smiled reminiscently. 'Ours. We lived in our grandparents' tiny house in a rundown neighbourhood but suddenly it was worth a fortune. Connie used her share to travel. I invested mine and got a job in the city, learning finance.'

'And never looked back.'

Caro marvelled. From troubled teen to billionaire took a lot of doing.

'Oh, I had setbacks. But I found mentors and learned from my mistakes.'

Jake made it sound something anyone could do. Caro thought of herself, all those years giving in to her father, not even able to look after her own baby—

'Hey.' He cupped her chin. 'What is it?'

Her heart turned over at his gentle touch.

'Nothing. Except that I'm incredibly impressed.' She tugged in a sharp breath. She'd avoided the inevitable for too long. Time to confront it. 'What did you want to talk about? You said it was time to leave.' Caro was proud of her even tone. 'Where will you go?'

'Somewhere to make a home for Ariane. I'd thought of St Ancilla, till your father...' He lifted those bare shoulders and Caro followed the movement, remembering how she'd clung to that broad expanse when they made love. 'Maybe Australia or—'

'Australia!' Caro's voice hit a shrill note. 'If you take Ariane I'll never see her.'

He dropped his hand. Caro's heart dropped too.

'Unless you come with us.'

'Sorry? You want me to move to Australia?'

'Or somewhere else. I'm open to suggestions. Somewhere we can make a home for Ariane.'

We. Her heart thundered. He'd said *we.*

'What, exactly, are you suggesting, Jake?'

He hesitated and to her surprise, Caro saw uncertainty on his face. It couldn't be. This was the man who'd stalked through a royal ball like an avenging angel intent on retribution, uncaring of scandal. Who'd spirited her away from her father and kept her safe from his machinations. Jake didn't do uncertain.

'We could bring Ariane up together.'

She couldn't think of anything she'd like more. Her pulse tripped and she had to stifle a surge of elation. It didn't seem possible.

'Together, not taking turns looking after her?'

'I want her to have stability and a loving family.' He paused, his long fingers squeezing hers. 'We could be that family.'

Caro tried to speak but the words stopped in her chest. She told herself to breathe, think this through, not jump to conclusions. Yet her heart leapt.

Less than twenty minutes ago she'd had a revelation, discovering the reason Jake affected her so profoundly.

Because she loved him. She'd fallen completely, devastatingly in love with Jake Maynard.

Her feelings for Mike hadn't been love, more excitement at escaping her restrictive life, the thrill of being wanted. He'd been her first crush. And he'd cured her of crushes for life.

Till Jake. Honourable, protective, tender, funny. He was everything she hadn't dared hope for. And now he talked about them making a family.

Because he'd fallen in love too? Excitement scudded through her.

Jake leaned in, warmth in his eyes. 'We could make it work, Caro. A marriage of convenience for Ariane's sake. What do you say?'

CHAPTER FOURTEEN

JAKE SAW THE fire in Caro's bright eyes die. It didn't flicker or fade. It was snuffed out in an instant.

In the same instant cold engulfed him.

Her lips thinned as she pressed them together. Within his grasp her hands jerked then stilled. She blinked once, twice, the dark pupils widening, making her look wounded, as if he'd hurt her.

Yet it was Jake who felt the punch to his gut, like a hunting knife jabbing flesh, piercing a vital organ.

He forced himself to breathe slowly. She was surprised. She wasn't rejecting him.

'It's a perfect solution, don't you see?' He sounded more confident than he felt. Like a desperate salesman giving a final pitch. That made him pause. He didn't do desperate. There was no reason for the anxiety gripping his belly.

'I realise it's an unusual solution to our situation.' Actually it was perfect. 'But think about it. Ariane needs stability and a family to love her. We're that stability. We give her that love. Even after such a short time I see the difference since you came into her life. We can be all she needs. And we're good together, you know we are.'

Jake made himself stop. He wasn't a snake oil sales-man, pushing her into a purchase she'd regret. He knew she'd enjoyed this time together since leaving St Ancilla. It wasn't only her relief at leaving her father's kingdom, or even, he suspected, being with her daughter. Caro revelled in his company and his lovemaking. She'd been gratifyingly eager for both.

Yet Caro looked anything but eager as she slipped her hands from his and hitched the sheet high. She trembled so much Jake could see it.

The blade at his belly twisted, gouging deep.

Jake had never laid himself open to rejection by a woman. Not after being rejected time and again by his mother. He'd kept his relationships with women to simple sexual transactions. This was the first time he'd put himself on the line.

It was impossible she'd shun him.

Yet his pulse juddered as he looked for a sign of understanding and agreement.

'But…marriage?' She frowned as if marriage to him was some distasteful medicine.

'Why not?' He shrugged his bare shoulders, chilling now despite the warmth of the room, and wished he'd waited instead of rushing into this. Instead of getting the easy agreement he'd anticipated, he had the unnerving sensation her response wouldn't be an enthusiastic 'yes'.

Would he have done better dressed for business in his office, with Caro sitting on the other side of the desk? The idea was preposterous. Yet—

'Isn't it a bit extreme? Couldn't we share custody, six months with you and six with me?'

Something heavy shoved down through Jake's middle. Disappointment or something stronger? Because she didn't leap at his suggestion. He told himself they discussed a pragmatic arrangement, that she wasn't rejecting *him*.

'You said it yourself. If we live on opposite sides of the world one of us would miss seeing her when she's with the other. This way she gets both of us.'

And we get each other.

'Besides, if you're pregnant, wouldn't it be the best outcome?'

Any thought that argument would clinch the deal died as Caro's face leached of colour. It was like watching flesh and blood turn to parchment and it curdled the hope within him.

'You're covering all bases, aren't you?' Instead of admiring his foresight, it sounded oddly as if Caro resented his pragmatism.

'We have to be practical.' He waited for her to agree. When she said nothing he went on. 'Neither of us want to fight for Ariane in court.'

Finally, to his relief, she nodded. At least there was one thing on which they agreed.

'We need a solution for Ariane that will work for us both. Why not stay together? Build on what we already have? I can see it working.'

He could see it so clearly he had to bite his tongue from insisting she must too. It was the best, the only solution.

'Can you?' Her gaze held his. It wasn't the look of a happy woman. A woman offered security and caring, plus wealth beyond most people's imaginings. Offered *him*.

Suddenly, instead of a billionaire with the world

at his feet, Jake felt like someone else. Someone unwanted, never good enough even to hold his parents' attention.

The sensation lasted only a second but it rocked Jake to the core.

So when Caro thanked him politely and said she needed to think about it he merely nodded and stood, forcing himself to rise and walk away on stiff legs.

The sun was warm on Caro's face as she drank in the peaceful scene. White-topped mountains that now seemed like friendly guardians rather than sombre presences. The alpine meadow dotted with the season's first flowers was tranquil, the only sound her daughter's voice.

Caro inhaled the scent of meadow grass, listened to Ariane's chatter as she played with Maxim, and willed herself to feel happy.

She had so much to be thankful for. They were safe, they were together and they were far from her father's influence. He still sent irate messages but it seemed he had more on his mind than pursuing his errant daughter. Money troubles, said Jake, who'd made it his business to find out. Significant money troubles, which explained why her father hadn't done more than bluster about her absence.

Caro and Ariane were building a real bond, which grew stronger daily. It was more than she'd once dared hope for.

She owed Jake so much. He made this possible. He could have prevented her seeing Ariane till the legalities were sorted out but he wasn't that sort of man.

Unlike her domineering father, Jake didn't play with

people and their emotions for his own ends. He was decent, honest, reliable, and he cared for Ariane so much it was impossible not to love him for that alone.

As if Caro didn't love him anyway.

Her chest tightened painfully. It shouldn't be possible after so short a time but her feelings were clear. She loved him as surely as she loved her daughter.

How much longer would he wait for her answer?

How much longer could she pretend she didn't know how to reply?

Last week he'd offered her a convenient marriage as a solution to their tangled situation. Ariane would acquire a family. Caro and Jake would get to be with her permanently.

It was simple and workable.

Except Caro wanted more. She wanted someone to love *her* for herself.

She reminded herself she'd have Ariane's love. But she'd grown greedy. Having spent this time with Jake, she wanted it all. The physical intimacy and more besides. She wanted Jake to care for her, not as a co-parent but because she was unique, someone he didn't want to live without.

Not because she might carry his child.

Caro looked at the tiny daisies in her hands, the flower chain she was making crushed.

When she'd asked for time to think Jake's expression had turned wooden. She'd seen the shutters come down before he strolled away to dress. Since then there'd been a barrier between them. Even in bed, at the height of passion, when Caro was on the verge of blurting out her feelings as he drove her to peak after peak of pleasure, she was aware of something different in Jake. As if he held something of himself back.

Jake gave her everything except love.

She'd lived without love all her life. She could live without it now, especially as she had Ariane. Her daughter would grow to love her, Caro felt it in her bones.

In time, if she wanted, there'd be more children, and she'd love them too. She should take what she was offered and be content.

'What's wrong, Caro? You look sad.'

She turned to find Ariane regarding her solemnly. Though her daughter was brighter and more relaxed now, she was sensitive to negativity, still easily worried.

'Nothing at all.' Caro smiled. 'I was thinking how peaceful it is here.'

'Maxim likes it. He's not sure he wants to live somewhere else.'

'Somewhere else?'

The solemn little face nodded. 'I heard Uncle Jake and Neil. We're moving.' The little girl swallowed. 'Will you come too, Caro?'

And that, of course, put her personal woes into perspective. What was more important than Ariane?

Caro leaned in and cuddled her daughter. 'That's the plan, sweetie.'

So it was decided.

All Caro had to do now was tell Jake she'd accept his marriage of convenience.

She'd marry the man she loved, yet it felt as if she gave up her soul. She'd have to spend her life pretending not to love him. Learning not to care when he wearied of their passion and sought pleasure with other women.

Caro set her jaw and pushed her personal feelings aside. They weren't as important as Ariane.

An hour later, as Caro headed to Jake's office to tell him her decision, her phone rang. She'd tired of her father's staff calling her old number to harangue her and had changed it last week. Was it Zoe? This would save Caro calling to tell her there was no need for legal action.

'Hello?' Caro tried to sound bright and happy. But the smile she forced felt like a grimace.

'At last.' Her father's voice struck like a blow. Caro stumbled to a halt, her stomach churning. Once more he'd managed to get her private number! Before she could gather her wits he went on, his voice serpentine with venom. 'Don't even think about hanging up, Carolina, or I'll make your lover pay.'

The sun was sinking when Caro forced herself up from the window seat where she'd slumped. Every joint felt stiff, as if she'd aged a lifetime in an hour. Not that her father had stayed on the phone that long. His call had been brief but it had changed everything.

Earlier this afternoon she'd felt sorry for herself, on the verge of marrying the man she loved to make a family with him and her daughter.

She hadn't known how lucky she was!

Now that choice was denied her. She had to give Jake up and Ariane too. Her father had made that clear. He was a man who didn't make empty threats.

It didn't matter that Jake had done nothing wrong, had broken no law. If her father vowed to destroy him he would. Even if it took years, he'd manipulate the truth, plant evidence, bribe people, all that and more, to destroy Jake's reputation and his business. The King had the contacts and the lack of scruples to do it. He'd even threatened extradition to St Ancilla on trumped-up charges relating to the disbursement of Jake's sister's estate and alleged mismanagement of an investment scheme there. He'd ensure Jake didn't get a fair trial. Destroying his reputation would devastate his business.

Unless Caro gave up her daughter and returned, alone, to the palace.

He'd taken his time planning his revenge for the way she stood up to him. It was something he excelled in. How had she let herself forget that?

The threat had made her realise too that her father would continue to influence their lives, spreading poison that would eventually infect Ariane, unless she, Caro, gave her up. There'd be no escape and ultimately Ariane would suffer.

Caro's throat constricted but she refused to cry. Now, more than ever, she had to be strong.

She didn't know how she was going to walk away from Jake and Ariane but she had to believe her daughter would be fine without her, because she'd have Jake. It wasn't as if Ariane knew Caro was her mother. Now she never would. Caro would have to get Jake to promise that at least.

Yet, here in her room, the room she hadn't slept in since returning from St Ancilla, Caro wondered how she'd find the strength to do what she must.

But surely it was simply one step then another, like after Mike's betrayal. And when she'd believed her baby dead.

Drawing a deep breath, Caro took a step, then another, towards the wardrobe where her suitcase was stored.

Jake had waited long enough. The days had stretched out and still Caro hadn't given an answer. She drove him crazy.

She made love as ardently as before, yet their emotional connection had severed.

He'd given up being patient. It was time for answers.

Answers he got as he opened the bedroom door and saw Caro with her back to him, suitcase open on the bed.

For a second that seemed to last for ever his feet stuck to the floor. He couldn't move, could barely process what he saw. But only for a second. He crossed the room and she swung around.

There was a flash of something in her eyes. Relief? Pleasure? Something that made the bleakness inside ease and hope surge.

Then it disappeared. Those violet eyes turned dull and shadowed, dropping to his chin.

He knew why. She'd decided he wasn't good enough. Why marry a commoner when she had handsome aristocrats hanging off her every word? He'd seen them at the ball, panting after her.

The weight within his ribs crushed him. His lungs laboured. Jake had to force himself to stand still and not haul her to him and insist they could work this out.

'This is your answer?' Another time he'd have winced at the raw emotion in his voice. 'Were you going to tell me or just let me work it out when you vanished?'

She jumped at his lashing words and Jake was torn

between wanting to soothe her and wanting to make her hurt as he did.

Had he ever felt such pulsing, writhing pain? He had a hazy recollection of something similar as a kid. The day he'd come home from school to discover his mother had cleared out again. Jake shoved the memory aside. He'd given up caring about his mother. But he cared about Caro. He'd thought...

She lifted her face slowly, as if reluctant to face him.

'I was going to tell you. I'm sorry, Jake. But I...' She shook her head and her glorious hair, loose around her shoulders, shifted like a living thing, attracting all the light in the room. It was burnished in shades of blood and rust, like the metallic tang of defeat filling his mouth. 'I've given your suggestion a lot of thought but it won't work.' She opened her mouth as if to say more then paused. 'It's time I left.'

She turned away and reached for a blouse, folding it methodically.

That was all the explanation he deserved?

His anger notched higher and so did his determination. He never quit. Never gave up on something worth fighting for.

Jake snagged a rough breath, then another. This wasn't the end. He refused to let her go like this.

'So you're going to fight me for custody of Ariane.'

Caro jumped and the blouse fell to the bed. For a long time she stood, utterly still, though tension emanated from her. He felt it like waves pummelling him.

'No... I've decided that won't work.' She picked up the blouse once more and began folding it with excruciatingly slow movements. 'Ariane is better off with you. You're her uncle. She knows you, loves you.' Caro's voice wobbled alarmingly and Jake felt its echo reverberate inside him as a shudder of astonishment.

He couldn't be hearing this. It was impossible. After all she'd been through Caro would *never* contemplate renouncing her child.

'You're giving up your *daughter*? The daughter you wanted so desperately? So desperately you came here under false pretences. So desperately you stood up to your father?' Jake stalked across to stand behind her shoulder. She hitched an uneven breath as the fabric in her hands became a mangled ball. Jake felt like mangling something himself. 'I don't believe it.'

What was going on? Did she find him so repulsive she'd give up Ariane rather than stay with him?

He couldn't believe it. He knew Caro. Even if things weren't as good between them now, she'd proved again and again that she was attracted to him. He'd cherished hopes it was something deeper than attraction.

Those narrow shoulders straightened. Her chin lifted and he caught a glimpse of Caro's proud profile.

'I've made my decision.' A pause, a long pause, so fraught Jake sensed she struggled. But if this was hard, why not accept his proposal? 'Ariane will be happy with you. I know you'll look after her. With me…' Her shoulders rose. 'It's better if she grows up without any connection to my family.'

Jake pounced on the mention of her family, a glimmer of hope easing the raw ache in his gut.

Because he couldn't believe she'd spurn him otherwise? Was he so desperate?

The answer was a resounding yes. For days he'd been on tenterhooks, giving Caro space to decide. In that time one thing had become abundantly clear.

That he had his own reasons for offering marriage and they weren't confined to Ariane.

Jake needed more from Caro. Not convenience. Not a mother for his orphaned niece.

He needed Caro for himself.

She spread the blouse on the bed a third time, smoothing then folding it. But her hands shook. Jake stood so close he felt the tremors, heard her uneven breathing.

This took more from her than she wanted to admit.

'What is it, Caro?' His voice was husky, rough with emotion he struggled to leash. 'What's wrong?'

'Nothing.' Her movements quickened, the fold lines on the shirt askew, but she didn't stop, almost throwing it into the suitcase and reaching for another.

Jake wanted to make her look at him but he didn't dare touch her. Not yet. He feared that if he did he wouldn't let her go.

'Why not marry me and give Ariane the life we both want for her?'

The life we both want for ourselves.

'I made a mistake. I'm not cut out for motherhood. I need to—'

'Caro.' Her name was a caress as he closed his arms around her, pulling her gently back against him, revelling in the feel of her there, where she belonged, even if she was rigid with tension. 'Tell me what's wrong. I know something is. You're a terrible liar.'

He felt the sob rack her though she stifled it. Still she didn't relax. Instead her movements grew quicker, her breathing too, as she leaned away from his restraining hold, grabbing fistfuls of clothes and tossing them into the suitcase.

'Please, don't make this more difficult, Jake. I don't want to marry you. We'd make each other unhappy and that wouldn't be good for Ariane.'

'And if you're pregnant?' He slid his palm to her abdomen. He'd told himself he'd support her if there was a baby. In fact he was thrilled Caro might carry his child. He'd begun to imagine what the baby would look like, how it would feel in his arms.

'I won't be. The odds are against it.'

She spoke so softly he had to crane to hear. Which brought him to the spice and warmth scent of her skin. Jake closed his eyes and inhaled. That undid him.

'Sweetheart, tell me what's wrong. I promise we'll find a way to deal with it.' Jake didn't care that his voice revealed his feelings. 'I want you with me. You and Ariane.'

If she'd been tense before it was nothing to her iron rigidity now. It felt as if she didn't even breathe.

'No! It's impossible. We can't.'

But Jake was listening now, really listening. He didn't hear rejection but desperation. A woman who didn't care for him or her child wouldn't sound as if she were being torn apart.

Her pain wrenched at his vitals. He'd do anything to take the hurt away.

He kissed the curve where her shoulder met her neck and felt her instant response as if her knees gave way. He gathered her closer. Caro's breath became a sigh and instead of fighting his hold she angled her head a fraction to allow unfettered access.

Triumph rose. Relief so profound it almost overwhelmed him.

Jake lifted one unsteady hand, pushing her hair

aside, nuzzling that sensitive spot as she leant against him.

Even if she didn't feel the same way about him, he could work with that. He was determined, single-minded and patient when he needed to be. He'd *make* her love him if it took years.

'You want to be with me,' he murmured against her skin, feeling her shivers of response.

She tried to move away, but Jake was implacable. He needed to understand and it seemed the only way to learn the truth was when he weakened Caro's defences. Her words confirmed it.

'Let me go, Jake. Please. You're wrong, I don't want you.'

Her body told another story, as did her voice. She sounded desperate but not convincing. Scared rather than angry. Of what? Surely not of a future together?

'I don't believe you.'

She stilled.

'What happened, Caro? What are you frightened of?'

'I…' She shook her head as if she'd run out of lies to distract him.

Gently Jake turned her to face him. Her eyes were wide and her mouth a crooked line of pain but it wasn't rejection he saw in those purple-blue eyes. It was fear.

Surely not of him? Jake was processing the possibility when abruptly his mind clicked into action.

'It's your father, isn't it? He contacted you.'

The instant flare of her eyes told him he'd hit the truth.

Silently Jake cursed. He'd done everything he could to stymie the King's attempts to reach Caro and thought he'd succeeded. What he'd learned in that confrontation between father and daughter at the palace had horrified him. Now the man turned even more vicious and unstable. Not simply because Caro dared defy him but because the house of cards he'd built around himself was being swiftly and methodically exposed.

Jake hadn't hesitated to probe into the monarch's affairs. Between them, professional investigators and Jake's well-placed business associates had uncovered an unsavoury, not to mention illegal web of financial misappropriation and fraud. King Hugo regarded the public purse as his own, but the structures he'd used to hide his misdoings were crumbling under pressure.

'That doesn't matter.' Caro's face was drawn and tense. 'I can't live with you and Ariane—'

'I still don't believe you.' Her head jerked up and she looked him in the eye. 'You want to be with us but you're frightened.'

How he welcomed her spark of annoyance. Seeing her frightened made him desperate. 'Has anyone ever told you you're arrogant, Jake Maynard?'

As a diversion it might have worked, once, weeks ago before he'd got to know Caro. 'Yes. You have, and it's true. But I'm right. You can't lie to me, Caro, you're no good at it.'

It was true, despite her earlier masquerade. Deliberately, lifting his arms wide, he stepped back, giving her space, though it went against every instinct to release her rather than embrace her.

Jake needed her to trust him.

'Tell me what he said, Caro. Playing by his rules hurts all of us.'

Finally she nodded. 'He demanded I return. He wants me there, to marry someone he's chosen.'

'Or what?' Jake kept his voice even despite his building fury.

'Or he'll destroy you. He means it, too,' she said in a rush. 'He hates me for repudiating him and you for taking my side. He'll find a way to bring you down. He said he'd make it his mission, no matter how long it takes.' Caro reached for Jake, grabbing his hands as if to convince him by sheer force. 'He'll bring trumped-up charges against you, get someone to testify you broke the law in your financial dealings—'

'Is that all?' Jake threaded his fingers through Caro's, melding their hands.

'All? Don't you understand? He'll destroy your reputation and then your business! You don't know how devious he is, the lengths he'll go to.'

'Oh, I know.' He should have been prepared for this, but he'd thought there was no way the King could worry Caro here. 'What I don't know is whether you'd stay with me if it weren't for his threats.'

She shook her head, the picture of desperation. 'Jake, please, listen. He'll wreck everything you've worked for. I can't let him—'

'He won't, Caro. Because he's about to go under.' Jake willed her to focus on his words, not her father's threats. 'He's stolen funds and borrowed against assets that don't belong to him. He's dipped into the public purse on a huge scale.'

Finally she was taking it in. Her eyes grew huge.

'He got careless and some of us in the finance sector have been doing our own investigating.' Because he needed to protect Caro and Ariane. 'He's a spent force, Caro. Don't believe his bluster. This is a last-ditch effort to save himself through you. My guess is he thinks I'll call off the creditors if he has you in his clutches. Believe me, he can't touch you. I promise.'

His pulse thundered through the silence and he watched as, gradually, the fear eased from Caro's face. If Jake had had any doubts about her belief in him, the fact that she took his word now proved otherwise. It warmed him from the inside out in a way only Caro could.

'*You* did all that? But why?' She frowned. 'You didn't know he'd threatened you.'

Seeing her puzzlement, Jake realised how alone she must have felt all those years. Had there ever been anyone to stand beside her? He swallowed, his throat constricting painfully. Her stoicism and determination really were phenomenal.

'You don't know?' Jake's voice stretched. He'd hoped she'd understand. 'For the same reason I hope you really want to marry me.'

His breath grew shallow, his lungs working overtime. No longer was he a savvy investor, a world-class businessman, secure in his success. Jake hovered on a knife edge between hope and disaster.

'I fell in love with you, Caro. I want you, not for Ariane but for myself.' He lifted her hand to his lips and allowed himself a fleeting kiss to her hand, taking courage from the throbbing pulse at her wrist. 'I know it's been a short time but I've never been more certain of anything.'

Jake watched emotions chase across her face, so fast he hadn't a hope of deciphering them. Her fingers shook in his grip.

'Caro?' His confident words deserted him. It emerged as a croak.

'You love me?' She shook her head and he slipped his other hand up to cup her cheek, holding her steady so she could read the truth in his eyes. 'It's not possible.'

'It is. That's why I took it badly when you needed time to think about marriage.'

'You said it was a marriage of *convenience*!' Jake heard her outrage and hurt and understood how badly he'd blundered with that impulsive proposal. But he'd been so excited at the idea he'd been unable to wait.

Now he had to get it right.

'It's taken me a while to confront what I feel. I'm not used to loving.'

Or being loved. His heart rose in his chest as he waited for her response.

'Nor am I.' Suddenly Caro was laughing, though it sounded ragged. And beautiful. 'I can't believe it.'

'It's true, absolutely true.' He stroked his thumb across her velvety cheek, watching her pupils dilate. 'What I don't know is how you feel about me.'

Their eyes locked and he felt that slam of connection, as real as a fist to his heart.

'Even when I hated you that night of the ball, I was afraid I loved you too.' Her words were magic, her expression mesmerising. 'Since then…it's been so hard feeling the way I do about you and thinking you didn't reciprocate. I don't know how I came to love you, Jake, or when, but I do. Totally. You devastated me when you offered a convenient wedding. I thought you only cared about Ariane, not me.'

Jake was filled with mingled pain and ecstasy, torn between exultation and regret.

He was spellbound by her luminous joy that belied the hurt she described.

Caro loved him!

His face split with a grin and he felt like whooping. Or kissing her senseless, except he needed more of her beautiful, wonderful words.

He planted her hand on his chest where his heart danced to a rackety beat and looped his arm around her, drawing her close where she belonged.

'Caro, I'm sorry. I'm better with numbers than emotions.'

'You're wrong, Jake. I've seen you with Ariane. I know how deeply you feel about her.'

'Not just about Ariane.' He revelled in the feel of her right here against him. With her hand on his chest she could feel his heart thundering out the truth. 'Will you be mine, Caro, for ever? I need you.' To his surprise, Jake discovered the admission, far from weakening him, made him feel stronger than he'd ever been.

'But my father...'

'Trust me to deal with your father.' Jake would let nothing come between him and the woman he loved. 'He's going under, Caro. He won't be in a position to threaten any longer.'

'Of course I trust you.' Her free hand slid to his shoulder, her grip firm and possessive. He loved it.

'So you'll marry me,' he pressed. He wanted everything clear between them, despite the urgent need to taste and caress her.

Her smile turned from misty to mischievous and he loved that too. 'Do you always negotiate this hard?'

'Only when our happiness is at stake. I won't allow anyone to stand in the way of that, king or no king.' What Jake felt for Caro, and what he saw shining in her expression, were too precious to abandon.

Caro's smile died and she rose on tiptoe, cradling his face in her palms. 'I love you, Jake.' The words filled him with awe and gratitude. 'If you're really sure...the answer is yes, because I don't think I can live without you.'

Jake drew his first easy breath in days. Caro was his. She loved him and they had all their lives to be together.

With a groan of release he gave in and covered her lips with his. Caro was as eager as he, kissing him back with all the fervour, all the caring a man could want. Jake sank into her, losing himself and finding more, far more. Together they were magnificent, one entity forged of trust, respect and love. He'd never felt so strong, so blessed. Gratitude vied with desire.

When, finally, they pulled apart enough to haul air into starved lungs, Jake looked down into a face made even more beautiful because of the gift they shared.

'You make me the happiest man in the world, Caro.' Maybe other lovers said it too. All Jake knew was that no one meant it more than he. 'Let me make you just as happy.'

EPILOGUE

'THERE YOU ARE! I followed the giggles.'

Caro spun around in the shallow end of the infinity pool overlooking the blue Pacific Ocean. There he was. Jake. Her lover, her man, her husband. Just back from meetings in the city, he'd shed his jacket and tie and was rolling up his sleeves as he crossed the flagstones.

Their eyes met and, as ever, she felt that hard pump of blood as if their hearts realigned to beat in sync. He smiled the slow, sexy smile that undid her as easily as his deft hands undressed her each night.

'Uncle Jake!' Ariane squealed and splashed out of the pool to cling to his legs. 'We waited and waited for you.'

Jake lifted his niece onto his hip, regardless of her wetness. Ariane's heart gave a great thump as she saw them together, the big man and the adoring little girl, bonded by a love so strong sometimes Caro had trouble believing this was real. Their family was better than any fantasy.

'Sorry, sweetie. But I have to work sometimes.'

Jake had reduced his hours, but their home on Sydney's exclusive northern beaches allowed him to commute to the city occasionally. Very occasionally. Mainly he worked from home, or delegated.

'Did you have a good day?' He bent his head towards the little girl and Caro smiled as Ariane described her day in detail. The withdrawn child she'd met in Switzerland was gone. Now Ariane was confident, secure and adventurous, already making friends with other local children.

Caro got out of the pool and went to fetch a towel, but Jake got in the way.

'Haven't you forgotten something important, Caro?' Ebony eyebrows lifted over teasing eyes.

'Well, if you don't mind getting even more wet…' She leaned close, kissing him soundly. When she pulled back he was grinning. His eyes held a promise that sent anticipation sizzling all the way to her toes.

'You're not listening, Uncle Jake. We have a surprise.' Caro blinked at Ariane's words. When Jake looked at her that way…

'A surprise?'

Her daughter nodded importantly. 'A visitor.'

Jake's eyebrows rose and Caro clarified. 'A visitor tomorrow.'

Ariane nodded. 'But I want to look for a book to share with him. Can I go now? Please?'

Fifteen minutes later, leaving Ariane dry, dressed and sorting her picture books, Caro returned to the terrace with its ocean views. The view had never looked so good as now with Jake powering through the pool wearing only surf shorts.

'A visitor?' He waded to the edge of the pool and stood between her knees as she sat with her feet in the water. Jake pressed a luscious kiss to the base of her neck. Caro's nipples pebbled and her thoughts frayed.

'Mm hm.' She tilted her head so he could nip his way up her neck to that spot below her ear that drove her insane. 'Paul.'

'Paul?' His voice was a husky whisper.

Caro planted her hands on Jake's wet shoulders and leaned back. She couldn't kiss and think. 'King Paul of St Ancilla. We invited him, remember?'

The last couple of months had been dramatic with her father bowing to pressure and abdicating in favour of his eldest son. There'd been some scandal but the full depths of the old man's deceit and theft hadn't been made public. The ex-King had quietly retired to a small estate on a distant island. The public didn't know he'd been banished. Meanwhile Jake helped Caro's brother work to restructure the royal debt with an ambitious plan of reinvestment and repayment. No one had the stomach for unseating a monarchy and destabilising a nation, so long as the man responsible was out of the equation.

'You're happy with that?' Jake's silvery eyes turned piercing.

'I said so before, didn't I? Paul could do with some time out, away from the court and the press.' And his mother and fiancée, though she didn't say that. Caro guessed neither of the women were particularly supportive but the way Paul had stepped up to his responsibilities, his honesty and genuine concern at their father's wrongdoing, had impressed her.

'The press will follow him here.'

Caro shrugged. 'I'll cope. I'm used to it, remember. Besides, if we accept his invitation and spend part of each year in St Ancilla we'll be in the spotlight even more.' She cupped Jake's harsh, handsome face in her palms. 'Are *you* sure you want to take that on? Associating with royals. Going to balls and such?'

'It's your home and your heritage, Caro, and Ariane's. I can cope if you can.' The glint in Jake's eyes grew wicked, turning her insides liquid. 'I enjoyed my first royal ball enormously.'

'It wasn't the ball but what came after.'

'I have a weakness for princesses.'

Caro huffed in mock dismay. 'Then you can't go to royal events. Who knows what princesses and duchesses there will be, even queens?'

Jake's expression made her pulse stutter. 'How could I notice them, Caro, when you've shown me what love is? You're Queen of my heart.'

That organ rolled over, beating frantically against her ribs. 'Sometimes I think you're too good to be true, Jake Maynard.' Her words were husky with love.

'I *know* you are, Caro. Which is why I intend to do everything I can to make you happy. Now come here and kiss me.'

* * * * *

If you fell in love with
Revelations of a Secret Princess,
you're sure to adore these other stories
by Annie West!

The Greek's Forbidden Innocent
Wedding Night Reunion in Greece
Sheikh's Royal Baby Revelation
Demanding His Desert Queen

Available now!

#3805 THE SPANIARD'S SURPRISE LOVE-CHILD
Passion in Paradise
by Kim Lawrence
Softhearted Gwen had always dreamed of the day tycoon Rio would discover their child. Yet the reality is astounding! Because when the brooding Spaniard sweeps back into her life, he demands their daughter—and her!

#3806 MY SHOCKING MONTE CARLO CONFESSION
Passion in Paradise
by Heidi Rice
He's Monaco racing royalty and I, Belle Simpson, was his housekeeper. But that evening, Alexi's searing gaze exhilarated me. Five years later, I finally have the chance to reveal my secret—Alexi's a father!

#3807 A BRIDE FIT FOR A PRINCE?
Passion in Paradise
by Susan Stephens
Samia's thrilled by the longing Prince Luca awakens within her but knows a temporary fling is their only option. A future with him is impossible. For the shadows of her past make Samia wholly unsuitable...don't they?

#3808 A SCANDAL MADE IN LONDON
Passion in Paradise
by Lucy King
Kate is *mortified* when billionaire Theo discovers her secret dating profile. Yet she can't resist his tantalizing offer to introduce her to pleasure beyond her wildest imagination! But the biggest scandal of all is yet to happen...

_____

Did she realize that every time she spoke to him, she tilted toward him? Did she realize that she fidgeted her way through every conversation? Was she aware that her breath hitched whenever he walked past her? Was she aware that at that very moment her hands trembled?

"The next thing I wanted to discuss is the kitchen," she said, moving the conversation on.

"What about it?" he asked lightly.

She tugged at the sheets of paper he'd placed his backside on. "You're sitting on my notes."

"My apologies." Sliding smoothly off the desk, he went and sat on the chair on the other side of her desk. "Is this better?" But she didn't respond. Her eyes were on his, wide and stark, her fidgety body suddenly frozen. "Helena?"

She blinked at the mention of her name and quickly looked down at her freed notes.

"Yes. The kitchen." Despite Helena's best efforts, her voice sounded all wrong.

It had been hard enough to breathe with Theo propped on her desk beside her—when he'd first perched himself there, she'd feared her heart would explode out of her chest—but when he'd moved off, she'd had to fist her hands to stop them from grabbing hold of him. Now he was sitting opposite her and she'd caught a sudden glimpse of his golden chest beneath the collar of his polo shirt, and in the breath of a moment her insides had turned to mush.

It shouldn't be like this, she thought despairingly. She'd spent three months under Theo's intoxicating spell, riding the roller coaster of her life.

He'd had the ability to make her forget everything that mattered. Under his spell she'd believed all she needed was Theo in her life to be happy. She was sure her mother had once believed the same thing before she'd sold her soul to a monster. Theo wasn't a monster like Helena's father, but his power over Helena had been just as strong.

How could she still react so strongly to him? She'd believed the sudden detonation of their relationship had killed her feelings for him, but she saw now that she'd been hiding them, hiding them so deep inside that she'd forgotten how powerful they were until one look at him in the Staffords boardroom had seen them poke their heads out from dormancy. Now the old feelings were slapping her in the face, taunting her, and it was getting harder and harder to fight them.

Eyes now determinedly fixed on the papers on her desk, she rubbed the nape of her neck, cleared her throat and tried again. "We need to discuss the kitchen's layout. Do you still want to consult a professional chef about it?"

She knew the moment she said it that she'd made a mistake.

Something sparked in his eyes. He leaned forward a little, a satisfied smile spreading over his face. "You do remember."

"Only that neither of us can cook." She quickly fixed her gaze back on her notes, aware her face was flaming with color.

"But you asked—specifically—if I still wanted to consult a chef about the kitchen... What else do you remember?"

She tucked her hair behind her ear and wrote something nonsensical on her notepad. "Have you a chef in mind to consult?"

"Answer my question."

Her hand was shaking too much to write anything else.

"Helena."

"What?" Helena intended for her one-syllable question to come out as a challenge. She might have succeeded if her voice hadn't cracked.

"Look at me," he commanded.

Heart thrashing wildly, she breathed deeply before slowly raising her face. "What?"

His voice dropped to a murmur. "What do you remember?"

Trapped in his stare, she found herself unable to lie. "Everything."

Don't miss
His Greek Wedding Night Debt
available April 2020 wherever
Harlequin Presents books and ebooks are sold.

Harlequin.com

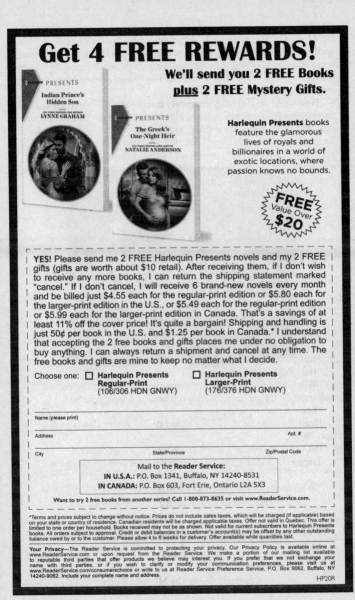

2729

**IF YOU ENJOYED THIS BOOK
WE THINK YOU WILL ALSO LOVE**

**⊕ HARLEQUIN
DESIRE**

*Luxury, scandal, desire—welcome to
the lives of the American elite.*

Be transported to the worlds of oil barons, family dynasties,
moguls and celebrities. Get ready for juicy plot twists,
delicious sensuality and intriguing scandal.

6 NEW BOOKS AVAILABLE EVERY MONTH!

HDXSERIES2020